BISON FRONTIERS OF IMAGINATION

THE GREAT ROMANCE

A Rediscovered Utopian Adventure

THE INHABITANT

EDITED BY DOMINIC ALESSIO

University of Nebraska Press: Lincoln and London

Portions of the introduction originally appeared in "Close Encounters of the Earliest Kind: A Postcolonial Sighting of Aliens from the Planet Venus and the First Human Colony in Science Fiction," *ARIEL* 33, no. 1 (January 2002), reprinted by permission of the Board of Governors of the University of Calgary; "The Great Romance, by The Inhabitant," *Kōtare* 2, no. 2 (November 1999): 3–17; and "*The Great Romance*, by The Inhabitant," *Science Fiction Studies* 20, no. 3 (November 1993): 305–40. Introduction © 2008 by Dominic Alessio.
All rights reserved.
Manufactured in the United States of America ⊗
Set in Bulmer by Kim Essman.
Designed by Ashley Muehlbauer.

Library of Congress Cataloging-in-Publication Data
Inhabitant, fl. 1881.
The great romance : a rediscovered utopian adventure /
The Inhabitant ; edited by Dominic Alessio.
p. cm. *The surviving two volumes of The Inhabitant's utopian science fiction story first published in Ashburton,*
New Zealand in 1881. Includes bibliographical references.
ISBN-13: 978-0-8032-5996-6 (pbk. : alk. paper)
1. Utopias—Fiction. I. Alessio, Dominic. II. Title.
PR9639.2.I65G74 2008   823'.8—dc22   2007037449

To my children,
Luca and Imogen,
who remind me how rewarding
it is to ask questions.

Contents

Acknowledgments	ix
Introduction	xi
A Note on the Text	lxi
The Great Romance, volume 1	1
The Great Romance, volume 2	61

Acknowledgments

In preparing this text for republication I would like to thank the following: the Alexander Turnbull Library, Wellington, for granting me access to the sole copy of volume 1; the Hocken Library, Dunedin, for allowing me access to the only existing copy of volume 2 and for the efforts of Kirsten Thomlinson and Katherine Milburn, in particular, who proved invaluable in my attempts to identify The Inhabitant; Nancy Batty and Robert Markley at *ARIEL* magazine for their indispensable suggestions relating to postcolonial criticisms of the work; the Board of Governors of the University of Calgary for allowing me to reprint parts of my earlier article from *ARIEL*; Ian Conrich and the New Zealand Studies Association for their interest in all things New Zealand; R. D. Mullen who taught me how to simplify as I prepared for *Science Fiction Studies* my first *Great Romance*-related piece; Lyman Tower Sargent for keeping me updated on everything possibly connected with the book; Ray Hargreaves, Roger Robinson, Gary Tee, and Peter Whiteford in New Zealand for their enthusiasm and assistance; Douglas Millard at London's Science Museum for space-related technical queries; Tom Swanson, Sara Springsteen, and especially Terence Smyre at the University of Nebraska Press for their constant support and feedback; the faculty in the Department of Humanities and Social Sciences at Richmond the American International University in London, and in particular Michéle Cohen, Jessica Langer, and Frank Trew, for their friendship, comments, and help; my parents Antonio and Maria for their love and much-needed proofreading skills; and my wife, Sarah, for her patience and love, not to mention her laptop during the last stages of completion.

Introduction

Sexual relations with aliens; free love among men and women; time travel; telepathy; world-shattering weapons of mass destruction; an astoundingly sophisticated vision about the problems of space flight; the first-ever discussion of off-world colonization by humankind; an urbane encounter with a friendly and intelligent nonhumanoid species; as well as the earliest mention of spacesuits, spacewalks, airlocks, shuttle craft, and planetary rovers: these are just a handful of the cutting-edge features to be found in volumes 1 and 2 of *The Great Romance*. The two novelettes, respectively only fifty-five and thirty-nine pages in length, were published separately under the pseudonym of The Inhabitant in 1881 in Ashburton, New Zealand.[1] This technological sophistication combined with a relatively not-too-turgid prose style that is commonly found in many scientific romances of the late nineteenth century make for a remarkable read. Hence *The Great Romance*'s republication for the first time here within a single bound volume and with an extended critical introduction.

The Great Romance is an extraordinary written work for a variety of other reasons as well. First, it is possible that this work was the urtext for the frame story of Edward Bellamy's *Looking Backward: 2000–1887* (1888), the most widely read and, among the general public, most influential of all utopian literature—one whose impact "has often been ranked as second only to Karl Marx's *Das Kapital* (1867)."[2] This relationship with *Looking Backward* becomes more likely when *The Great Romance* is compared to Bellamy's 1889 short story, "To Whom This May Come," on which its influence appears pervasive.[3] Second, *The Great Romance* is another indicator of just how widespread the writing and publishing of science fiction and utopian literature was in the nineteenth century. In particular it reaffirms a distinct antipodean tradition particular to New Zealand that includes the work of other well-known authors such as Samuel Butler, Jules Verne, and Anthony Trollope. Third, *The Great Romance* is one of the first works in the history of science fiction to provide a nondidactic depiction of an overtly alien species. The treatment that the "Venuses" receive, although paternalistic and laced with late-Victorian eugenic and Darwinian ideas, is sympathetic in nature. This rather benevolent depiction of intelligent alien life puts the work ahead of its time, since most contemporary science fiction novels (post–*The Great Romance*) generally tend to depict alien creatures as overtly threatening bug-eyed monsters. Finally, since alien species in science fiction are, as a rule, parabolically displaced in time and space by a postcolonial "Other" (such as the indigenous Maori peoples in *The Great Romance*), the attitude toward aliens and colonization presented in volume 2 not only illustrates a complicated late nineteenth-century British imperialist, racist, and militarist zeitgeist, it simultaneously serves to underline the more enigmatic and unique attitudes expressed by Pakeha (European) settlers toward the Maori people of New Zealand. Such an attitude makes the history of colonization in that former colony different from the history of contact with indigenous peoples in the rest of the British Empire. As M. P. K. Sorrenson reiterates with regard to this more distinctive European attitude in New Zealand, "The conflicts that resulted from European colonisation had much in common with frontier conflicts in other colonies—but there were also some marked differences. While in Australia 'the Aboriginal was despised as a rural pest,' in New Zealand 'the Maori was respected as a warrior.'"[4]

For all these reasons, *The Great Romance* not only ranks with the well-known New Zealand–based science fiction and utopian texts from the turn of the century—such as Samuel Butler's *Erewhon* (1872) and Julius Vogel's *Anno Domini 2000; or, Woman's Destiny* (1889)—but also deserves mention alongside some of the contemporaneous and more renowned science fiction texts of the European and American metropolitan world. Such an achievement is even more remarkable when one considers that this work was published in a small South

Introduction

Island agricultural town that even today boasts fewer than fifteen thousand inhabitants.⁵

Although published separately as two novellas, volume 1 can be further divided into two parts. It begins with the account of nineteenth-century protagonist John Brenton Hope who, after waking in a geographically unspecific location in the year 2143 following a deliberately induced chemical sleep initiated in a future 1950, discovers a wonderfully advanced society replete with mechanical marvels, immense orderly metropolises, telepathy, space travel, and a romantic love interest in the form of a beautiful young woman named Edith Weir. In what can be called the second part of volume 1 (which begins with chapter 8), Hope journeys to the planet Venus with two male companions, Alfred Weir (Edith's brother) and their mutual friend Charles Moxton. Their means of transportation is the scientifically advanced spaceship *Star Climber*. The purpose of their mission is to sound out the planet for future human settlement. Volume 1 ends with a landing on a very Earth-like Venus and the subsequent exploration of the new world. Volume 2 follows the story of Hope's companions' return to Earth in order to report their discoveries and to begin the transportation of human colonists, including Edith, back to Venus. During this return journey Weir accidentally remains adrift in space after the *Star Climber* makes an unplanned landing on a meteor; he literally falls off the face of this small peripatetic world. In the meantime Hope, who has been left on Venus to further explore the planet by himself, encounters a sentient, and by-all-appearances friendly, alien couple. The novel ends abruptly with Hope's quest to find other Venuses. It is not known whether a volume 3 was ever written and, if so, if it still exists.

PROVENANCE AND AUTHORSHIP

Volume 1, although neglected until recently, was included in A. G. Bagnall's *National Bibliography of New Zealand to the Year 1960* and Lyman Tower Sargent's bibliography of New Zealand utopian literature.⁶ The only known original of the work exists in the Alexander Turnbull Library in Wellington. Volume 2 was assumed to have never been written or lost until it was rediscovered during the mid-1990s at the Hocken Library in Dunedin. Apparently it had once formed part of Dr. Hocken's original collection.⁷ There is no listing of either novella in the National Library of New Zealand/ Te Puna Mátauranga O Aotearoa, the British Museum, the British Library, or the U.S. Library of Congress catalogs. Both volumes are briefly mentioned in *The Oxford Companion to New Zealand Literature*, which points out that *The Great Romance* exhibited "considerable scientific acumen."⁸ The mention, however, is found under the general rubric of science fiction, and the work neither merits a separate entry nor includes discussion of how innovative it was. As far as international literary criticism is concerned, only volume 1 is mentioned in *The Encyclopedia of Science Fiction*, albeit briefly as "NZ's first space story."⁹ Subsequent discussions examining various significant aspects of the work have also appeared in the journals *Science Fiction Studies*, *Kōtare*, and *ARIEL*.¹⁰

With regard to authorship, only the pseudonym "The Inhabitant" is given, a description quite common at the time for guidebooks in both the United Kingdom and the United States. The choice of nomenclature appears appropriate since the work purports to be, in part, a kind of guidebook from the perspective of a future traveler. As to the identity of the author, nothing further is known, although in his *National Bibliography*, Bagnall states without explanation that the writer was one "Honnor of Ashburton." Dr. Hocken's annotation in the Hocken Library also mentions this same author. A search of various New Zealand databases identified one Henry Honnor who had settled in Dunedin in 1858 but was listed as a carpenter by profession. In the 1880s a Henry Honor (with a single *n*) was also apparently working as a carpenter in Blenheim, two hundred miles to the north of Ashburton. To compound the mystery of the author's identity, yet another Henry Honor, this one from New Plymouth, also owned land in the Ashburton vicinity.¹¹ Furthermore, two farmers by the name of Herbert Honour and Henry Honour are listed in the 1880–1881 Ashburton Electoral Roll.[12] Unfortunately, there is no evidence linking the Dunedin-based Honnor, or any other Honors or Honours, to the text.

Most recently, Garry Tee at the University of Auckland has joined the fray, suggesting that the introductory dedication to John Keats in volume 1, for which there is no explanation and no obvious link with the story itself, is similar to another sonnet dedicated to Keats that was also published in Dunedin in 1881. According to Tee, its author was local solicitor Ebenezer Storry Hay (1850–1887), who wrote under the pseudonym "Fleta." Although Tee suggests it is highly unlikely "that two people would both have published, in Dunedin in 1881, poems dedicated to John Keats," there is no direct evidence to definitively link Hay with *The Great Romance*.[13] Unfortunately, the destruction by fire of the *Ashburton Guardian*'s offices has made it impossible to check old records. In an attempt to identify The Inhabitant, searches have also been conducted of various Dunedin newspapers from 1881, including the *Otago Daily Times*, *Echo*, *Illustrated New Zealand Herald*, and *Saturday Advertiser*, as well as the literary sections of the *Otago Witness*, all to no avail.[14] The only known contemporaneous reference to the novellas is an anonymous review that appeared on page 1 of the *Otago Daily Times* of February 18, 1882, which alludes to the volumes being the work of "a young writer."[15] We are left, like Pirandello's *Six Characters in Search of an Author*, with a text without an ending and no clear idea about the identity of the author.

THE INFLUENCE ON BELLAMY

Questions of authorship and the existence of a third volume aside, *The Great Romance* would be worthy of attention in its own right in the history of utopias and science fiction for its possible influence on *Looking Backward*. Bellamy's novel recounts the tale of a wealthy Bostonian who, having fallen asleep in the year 1887, awakens in

Boston in the year 2000 to see a wonderfully advanced society that had resolved, by way of nationalization, all the problems plaguing the industrializing nineteenth-century world. Partly because of the story line (especially the protagonist's psychological struggle to come to grips with awaking in a future society), and partly because of the timing of his vision (in a world struggling to accommodate the effects of rapid industrialization), the novel went on to become an international best-seller. Bellamy's Cabet-like clarion call went on to affect, in varying degrees, the Populist Party in the United States, the Fabians in Britain, revolutionaries in Russia, Zionists in Europe and Palestine, and labor leaders throughout the British settlement colonies. His optimistic vision of the future is reported to have also directly influenced numerous writers and thinkers, including Charles Beard, Anton Chekhov, Eugene Debs, Maxim Gorky, George Bernard Shaw, Leo Tolstoy, and H. G. Wells. By 1900 it had also generated more than fifty other utopian responses, the most notable being William Morris's *News From Nowhere* (1890).

The Great Romance and *Looking Backward* hold an intriguing number of similarities, suggesting that the former may have been the inspiration for the latter. Although varieties of stories about suspended animation, such as the twenty-year sleep in Washington Irving's "Rip Van Winkle" (1820), were a literary contrivance used well before the late nineteenth century, the narrators of both novels (Hope in *The Great Romance* and Julian West in *Looking Backward*) awake after especially long sleeps—193 years for Hope, 113 for West. When Hope awakens he sees a strange man, who appears to be a mesmerist, staring at him. West, too, was put to sleep by a mesmerist. Both narrators fall in love with women named Edith, who coincidentally happen to be descended from the narrators' friends in their original time periods. In *The Great Romance* Edith Weir is descended from Hope's closest friend, John Malcolm Weir; in *Looking Backward* Edith Leete is the great-granddaughter of West's nineteenth-century fiancée, Edith Bartlett. Both Ediths are, not surprisingly, additionally described as dazzlingly attractive. Hope's Edith "swept completely all other thoughts or imaginations, joys, or sorrows, from [his] heart" (vol. 1, pp. 12–13; subsequent references here will use a similar but abbreviated format). West's Edith is "the most beautiful girl [he] had ever seen."[16] Furthermore, both Ediths act as cicerones for Hope and West in their respective future worlds.

A further likeness between *The Great Romance* and *Looking Backward*, although one common to other fantastic tales, is that both authors assume the future will be, to quote The Inhabitant, a "GOLDEN AGE" (1.12). The cities of the twenty-first and twenty-second centuries are depicted as the apotheosis of an urban planner's dream. When Hope is first shown the cityscape of the future he sees "an immense city" where "the streets were as thickly peopled as the old London streets, but they were four times their width and planted with trees along either side" (1.16). West's description of Boston in the year 2000 is similar: "At my feet lay a great city. Miles of broad streets shaded by trees and lined with fine buildings . . . stretched in every direction."[17]

Where the two works differ is in intent. The Inhabitant appears primarily concerned with producing an entertaining read packed with a number of remarkably sophisticated technological visions. The text might have simultaneously doubled as a promotional piece aimed at attracting European settlers and visitors to colonial New Zealand. The reader simply has to substitute the overcrowded Earth of the twenty-second century for Europe of the nineteenth century, and a Venus full of wildlife, natural resources, and the odd friendly "native" for colonial New Zealand, for the booster intent of the novelette to become readily apparent. The Inhabitant even includes kangaroo-like animals as one of Venus's exotic species, although kangaroos, which are unique to Australia (and not New Zealand), also appeared as Martian animals in Percy Greg's pivotal 1880 science fiction work, *Across the Zodiac*, where they functioned as exotic proxies. It is possible, too, that rather than knowingly operating as a booster piece, *The Great Romance* may merely have been drawing upon the wealth of ideal imagery that had already been used to promote the young and distant colony.[18]

Nevertheless, if *The Great Romance* had been conceived primarily as a promotional device, it was certainly not the only New Zealand utopian work to do so. Elements of former premier Julius Vogel's utopian novel, *Anno Domini 2000; or, Woman's Destiny* (1889), also read like advertisements to promote the country, especially those relating to the healing properties of the country's thermal baths.[19] On occasion the association of the nation with the fantastic may have been deliberately made in order to promote the country, as in George Bell's *Mr. Oseba's Last Discovery* (1904), which tells the story of an inhabitant from the center of the world who discovers utopia in New Zealand. It has been said that this text, which includes fulsome landscape descriptions and praise for New Zealand's trailblazing politics as well as photographs of some of New Zealand's politicians and scenic sites (many of which are entirely unconnected to the book), could have been underwritten by New Zealand's Tourist and Publicity Department in order to deliberately encourage tourism and investment.[20]

In contrast to the potential promotional appeal of *The Great Romance*, the agenda of Bellamy's novel, although also propagandistic, appears to be the ideological polar opposite, namely, to emphasize the need for a socialist transformation that would end "the old laissez-faire capitalist order" and transform America "into an orderly society based on cooperation and social harmony."[21] Bellamy's work is not, therefore, a glorified real estate advertisement. According to Paul Alkon, author of *Science Fiction before 1900*, one of Bellamy's additional aims was to argue that an efficient use of advanced technology could "liberate people for retirement at age forty-five."[22] While this social agenda might seem a world away from *The Great Romance*, there is a hint of similar thinking when Hope proffers a vision of singing and vigorous workers who only needed "a few year's work in the early years of life" for there to be ample material provision for all of the technologically advanced Earth in the twenty-second century (1.25).

Stylistically the two works differ considerably. *The Great Romance* reads like a fevered dream in which The Inhabitant exhibits a passionate thirst for new experiences, an "appetite for the wonderful" (1.56) or an *innatus cognitionis amor* such as that expressed by Dante's Ulysses. Chapter 20 of his novella is even entitled "Exploring the Wonder." Bellamy's story functions as a more practical reality, his paradise being restricted to Earth, where progress is achievable and not already existent, as in some fairylike land of luxury. Unlike *The Great Romance*, therefore, the Boston of Bellamy's world offers a concrete blueprint for social action in this "reality" and does not necessarily depend upon a pseudoscientific turn in humanity's evolution.[23]

This emphasis upon evolutionary development raises a further significant difference between the two works, namely, the means by which these future utopias arise. Whereas The Inhabitant attributes the rise of utopia to the advent of telepathy, Bellamy envisions it as the result of nationalization. Consequently, telepathy plays no part in the cooperative Boston of 2000. Bellamy did, nonetheless, credit the rise of a utopian society to telepathy in his short story "To Whom This May Come." In that tale a shipwrecked narrator is rescued from a group of Pacific islands by telepathic inhabitants. Here, as in *The Great Romance*, the fact that all thoughts are public and wicked intentions cannot be concealed, has resulted in everyone having only honorable thoughts or those who have undesirable motives are isolated. In both telepathic stories the utopians are friendly and the narrator finds a guide to educate him about the society as well as a beautiful woman to love.

Tales involving the theme of immortality have been a traditional staple of classical writing since the ancient Sumerian epic *Gilgamesh*. In the same vein but in relation to interplanetary travel, a special sleeping drink was taken by humans to protect them from the vacuum of space in Johannes Kepler's 1609 tale *Somnium*. Suspended animation and other variants on the theme are also topics frequently alluded to in *The Great Romance* and they provide an important basis for the plot. However, these are not aspects of the text that appear to be satisfactorily developed or explained. Early on in the story Weir informs Hope that "amongst the younger men and women, the old idea of perpetual life is reviving" (1.9). A short time later, during a conversation with Weir's father, the latter warns him, "You are afraid to let nature take its course, you are strengthening your body with the perpetual elixir . . . hoping to give yourself a right to perpetual life" (1.30). Do Hope and some utopians desire to take the original sleeping draft again, or is there a new version of this potion extant that awards immortality without all the sleepy side effects? As if to support the latter, soon after landing on Venus the astronauts partake of their own stock of this "aqua vitae," an elixir which, according to Hope, if taken with "discretion" will allow humans to "outlive the very world" they inhabit (1.53).

A further weakness in the text, related to the theme of immortality, is an obscure and very brief indication from a future fictional *Punch* publication suggesting that Weir was not the only one to take a sleeping potion. What's more, the publication also indicates that both Weir and Moxton partook of a special chemical mixture. Moxton's concoction, though, is described as being "not so good" (1.6). A few lines later the Weir of the twenty-second century tells Hope that "your friend [the John Weir of Hope's century] left this world" (1.7). Some explanation as to why only Hope's potion seems to have worked might have been helpful. It is also somewhat unsettling, although never fully explained in the text, that for a great deal of Hope's time in suspended animation he was being subjected to psychic violation by whomever chose to read his thoughts. There had even been some discussion by these so-called advanced humans about terminating Hope's life.

Just as Bellamy may have borrowed elements of his novel from contemporary sources, the same appears true of *The Great Romance*, for a possible relationship also exists between it and the dystopian text *The Coming Race* (1871) by the English politician and novelist Edward Bulwer-Lytton (1803–1873). The connection between these two works deserves some comment. Not only do both deal with the evolution of the human race into a higher telepathic order but they also showcase the use of electromagnetic forces. The scenes in *The Great Romance* in which Moxton uses magnetism to control the movements of a stick and later to repel the clutch of a predatory flower are strikingly reminiscent of the rod used in *The Coming Race* to control what Bulwer-Lytton terms the "vril" (from which the British commercial name Bovril originated).

Although the "late nineteenth century saw a boom in occult romances featuring various kinds of extra-sensory perceptions," the fact that *The Great Romance* stresses that these ESP powers are the result of humankind's natural evolution—a factor only truly developed by science fiction writers of the twentieth century—serves to make this obscure and early New Zealand text all the more interesting.[24] Susan Stone-Blackburn, who discusses the treatment of psychic powers in early science fiction, calls Edward Bellamy's "To Whom This May Come" "a trailblazer in its exploration of effects telepathy might have on society and in its suggestion that under special conditions evolution might distil ancient and genuine but sporadic and unreliable human psychic abilities into universal and reliable ones."[25] It should now be evident that this trail was blazed not by Bellamy in 1889 but by The Inhabitant seven years earlier and that *The Great Romance* forms an important bridge between Bulwer-Lytton's *The Coming Race* and Bellamy's short story.

The Great Romance is not the first text that has been mentioned as a possible source for Bellamy's *Looking Backward*. Bellamy scholars, including his biographer, Arthur E. Morgan, have suggested that he may have borrowed some of his ideas from John Macnie's 1883 dystopian tale *The Diothas*, which was written just after *The Great Romance*. According to Morgan, in both *The Diothas* and *Looking Backward*, "the device of hypnotism was used . . . [and] the hero had a sweetheart named Edith. On waking from the long sleep in each case the hero fell in love with a distant descendant of 'Edith.' In each case, too, the father or guardian of the heroine, a man of exceptional intelligence and culture, became interpreter of the new world to the hero who had emerged from the nineteenth century. Each of these works foresees radio, television, automobiles, and other technical developments."[26]

As there is no direct evidence linking Bellamy with The Inhabitant's text, or even with New Zealand (which Bellamy never visited), a probable scenario—excluding an unlikely but not impossible situation in which Bellamy somehow came across a copy of *The Great Romance*—is that Macnie himself was influenced by the novella and he in turn influenced Bellamy. While there is also no proof that Macnie had read The Inhabitant's work or had even visited New Zealand, there does exist a substantial body of circumstantial evidence to link Macnie with the former colony. In *The Diothas* Macnie referred frequently to New Zealand, which he called "Maoria," and he also wrote a great deal about the progress that the colony had made over the centuries. Furthermore, the protagonist of his utopian story, Ismar Thiusen, was mentioned specifically as coming from the North Island of the country.[27] If Bellamy's biographer can suggest that there are enough similarities between *The Diothas* and *Looking Backward* to support the possibility that Bellamy may have borrowed some of his ideas from Macnie, and since the similarities identified between these two texts are virtually identical to those between *The Great Romance* and *Looking Backward*, it stands to reason that there might have been a relationship between Bellamy and The Inhabitant, albeit an indirect one.

SCIENTIFIC REALISM

While a number of space-travel stories were published earlier than *The Great Romance*, there were perhaps only a handful that provided so detailed and extensive an account of the difficulties involved, namely Jules Verne's *Autour de la Lune* (1869) and Percy Greg's *Across the Zodiac*. Otherwise many of these earlier works, according to David Pringle, "tended to turn a blind eye to the problems involved in moving outside the Earth's atmosphere."[28] Instead these early works are often credited with being "flights of fantasy using the journey itself

Introduction

and the Moon as allegory," where "the craft employed were little different from routine contemporary modes of transportation." In fact, "in one story, someone even walked to the Moon!"[29] By contrast *The Inhabitant*'s vision of the shape of things to come appears particularly credible, with one or two notable exceptions—such as the depiction of Venus as an Eden-like paradise with its own moon and the use of rapidly flapping wings to help power spacecraft. As such it reflects a nineteenth-century tendency to focus more and more "on the scientific and technical aspects of lunar and planetary voyages."[30] Subsequently, a number of pioneering technological aspects have been incorporated into the text by the author, and any analysis of *The Great Romance* must therefore discuss them at length. According to some critics it is specifically this technologically driven "novum" that distinguishes a story as belonging to the science fiction genre.[31]

One of the most startling innovations in the novella is the mention of the absence of gravity on a spaceship and a subsequent awareness of muscle fatigue. Although Joseph Atterley, writing under the pseudonym George Tucker, did discuss the effects of weightlessness in his speculative *Voyage to the Moon* (1827), and Greg described how "coffee, spilled from a cup, floats inside the space ship," at first, "many early authors did not realize that complete weightlessness is a consequence of free fall."[32] So *The Great Romance* appears immediately cutting edge on account of this innovation alone.[33] Intriguingly, *The Great Romance*, although it does not dwell on the effects a lack of gravity might have upon space travel, goes a step further than other contemporary works by considering, if only briefly, the physical impact that this weightlessness might have upon the human body. According to Hope, "During our voyage, where a hasty step would send you flying up against the roof, and even the heaviest things were without appreciable weight, our muscles had, despite our best endeavours, become relaxed and weakened" (1.52). Such attempts at realism were groundbreaking in 1881, as concerns about the medical effects of weightlessness on astronauts were only first introduced by the "father of space travel," Konstantin Tsiolkovsky

(1857–1935), in 1883. Nor were these issues even considered in the early 1930s by the British Interplanetary Society, an organization considered to be in the vanguard of space-travel studies during the interwar period.[34]

Another realistic scientific premise broached in the text, and one of which Greg was also aware, is the recognition of the problems that meteors and other assorted cosmic debris could inflict upon a spaceship. In *The Great Romance* this danger is ingeniously avoided, fictionally at least, by the *Star Climber* having a defensive cannon which, like the Death Star in *Star Wars* (Lucas, 1977), was powerful enough to destroy an entire moon. The *Star Climber* also has an "intense magnetic current" (1.34), which appears to function as a kind of force field. The recognition of the potential damage that the extreme heat generated by a planet's atmosphere could inflict on a space vessel during takeoff and reentry is also groundbreaking. Although Jules Verne had mentioned it in *Autour de la Lune*, it was a scientific concern not addressed until much later by the American rocket pioneer Robert H. Goddard (1882–1945) in the mid-twentieth century.[35] To prevent astronauts suffering from the effects of this heat, The Inhabitant also develops the concept of a spaceship designed with an onboard "cold air machine" (1.47).

The use of a planet's rotation and atmosphere to increase or decrease a space vessel's speed is also an idea formerly thought to have first been proposed by Goddard.[36] Yet once again *The Great Romance* got there first:

> Then there came a sudden roar, a huge swerve of our vessel, as under its influence we shot in again to the planet. Again we repeated the experiment, although I now had the command, and Moxton in the look-out. "Keep her in it," they both said, and we dipped down so close as well nigh to touch the feathery clouds; this was enough for us all; the heat we subsisted in for the next hour would have fairly cooked any dead substance. But as we got clear again and began to cool, we saw what an immense part of our speed we had lost. (1.47)

Introduction

Issues dealing with the verisimilitude of space flight do not end here. Problems of fresh air and monotony are addressed too, the former by bringing along vast stored quantities of oxygen and the latter by conducting scientific experiments while on board: "Our brains were tired with the inevitable inactivity. We were forced to take refuge in work" (1.37). Concerns regarding the latter might have derived from mid-nineteenth-century scientific studies of prolonged confinement that had been conducted on submarine crews.[37]

Although *The Great Romance* was published before Einstein developed his theory of relativity, there is a brief but beguiling reference to faster-than-light travel: "Were it possible that other vibrations could travel swifter even than the beams of the sun, unseen yet no less real" (1.43). Similarly, although Frank H. Winter credits Goddard as speculating in 1918 on human migration beyond the solar system, it appears as though The Inhabitant had conceived of such a possibility nearly four decades earlier[38]: "There seems to be no limit to the speed we might attain in space, and if so, then distance becomes annihilated, and the whole universe open to us. There are other suns, and doubtless around them systems of planets" (1.41).

The reasons why Venus is chosen as a potential destination for human colonization are worthy of note as well. Venus was a planet known to have an atmosphere and was therefore a good bet for having the ability to support life. Like Mars it had thus been considered by scientists in the late nineteenth century as a place on which life might exist, as it seemed to pass what modern astronomers refer to as the "Goldilocks test," namely that it is close enough to the Sun for water to remain a liquid yet not so close that any life would be burned to a cinder. Although Mars is not mentioned in *The Great Romance*, the Moon is dismissed as a potential site for human colonization since The Inhabitant is aware of its lack of oxygen (1.34). As the astronauts in *Star Climber* gradually approach Venus, the description they give of the planet, "like a moon at three-quarter's full" (1.43), is remarkably similar to photographs taken of Venus and other planets from space, once more demonstrating the visionary elements of the text. There is also an astonishing description of Venus that echoes later science fiction film images of planets viewed from up close in space: "There, hanging above us, as though it might suddenly fall and crush us into oblivion, hung the great planet, half in sunshine, half in shadow ... hanging right over our heads its clouds and waters, mountains and forests, spread out in wonderful state above us" (1.48).

The focus on Venus as a potential site for life also reflects the then-current scientific writing on pluralism—the belief that life might exist elsewhere in the universe. It demonstrates that the author was well versed with the most up-to-date astronomy-related discourses of the late nineteenth century. Richard Proctor, for example, whose *Other Worlds Than Ours* (1870) ran through several editions and printings, suggested "that all the evidence pointed to 'Venus as the abode of living creatures.'"[39] Likewise, the famous English astronomer Sir John Herschel (1792–1871) suggested that the clouds on Venus could indicate an alien existence on that planet.[40] It was only later—once Italian astronomer Giovanni Schiaparelli (1835–1910) reported *canali* (canals) on Mars and American astronomer Percival Lowell (1855–1916) began to popularize the concept of intelligent life there—that humankind's interest began to turn to the red planet instead.[41]

Although the *Star Climber* moves improbably by rapidly beating its wings, these are not its only means of momentum. Its defensive cannon can be swiveled and used for solid-fueled rocket propulsion, and in volume 2 its "rocket tubes" are mentioned (2.90). The description of the *Star Climber* leaving Venus even resembles the images and sounds from later twentieth-century rocket launchings: "The stream of fire flashed out and the fearful deafening roar fell upon my ear. I saw her rush, upwards, onwards, amid such a continuous thunder peal ... she left in fire and flame" (2.70).

The Inhabitant must also have been aware of the need to choose a suitable launch window prior to takeoff and to carefully take into consideration the alignment of the planets, a factor that Verne, too, had mentioned in his *De la Terre à la Lune* (1865). According to the astronauts in *The Great Romance*, "we must make exact observations and know our rate of speed; also how much we should need to alter our course, for we were not rushing on to a fixed spot, to an oasis in the desert of the heavens, but to a wandering star that was here and there, or still farther on, according to the hour at which you sought it. We could not rush madly on, or we should reach the place appointed weeks before the planet spun its immense mass thither" (1.40).

The Great Romance also holds the first-ever description of a spacesuit, making the novella avant-garde both in the scientific realm and the science fiction realm: "They prepared their air-pipe supplies—something like a bagpipe in appearance; they could breathe in the air through a mouthpiece.... With these on they could walk in a vacuum for an hour or more" (2.91). This spacesuit is also equipped with goggles that fastened tightly over the face "so that the atmosphere could touch no part of his body" (2.92). Intriguingly, the first reference to spacesuits and goggles that I have managed to track down is in the British Interplanetary Society's records of the 1930s, although Tsiolkovsky is credited with coming up with the idea sometime toward the end of the nineteenth century and the German rocket pioneer Hermann Oberth (1894–1989) speculated on the concept in the early twentieth century.[42] The depiction of spacesuits in the novella is also inventive. When Weir and Moxton walk outside the *Star Climber*, encountering for the first time a low-gravity environment, their movements clearly resemble the frustrations, dangers, and humor of the first Moon walks: "Don't fool about Weir. I believe a good jump would send one clear altogether" (2.91).

The author of *The Great Romance* also appears acutely aware of the need to maintain an airtight environment whilst onboard the spaceship. Consequently *The Great Romance* includes what could be another first in the history of science and science fiction: the use of an airlock. "The sliding doors [of the spaceship] were shot back and closed again behind them, then Weir opened the outer one and stepped out" (2.91). When the *Star Climber* lands on Venus the astronauts also exit the ship by way of "gangways" (1.52).

Both concepts, presumably borrowed from contemporaneous ships and submarines, went on to become staples of much later science fictional imaginings.

A further innovation in the text is the introduction of a kind of shuttle craft or lunar rover that is used by Hope to explore Venus. He calls it the *Midge*, and it is described simply as a kind of fantastic "boat" that can "run, or fly, or swim" (2.76). Although these types of vessels are now a mainstay of science and science fiction, such as the *Eagles* in *Space: 1999* or the *Galileo* and *Copernicus* in the original *Star Trek* (and not forgetting the real-life *Sojourner* on the NASA Mars Pathfinder mission), discussion of modular devices during space exploration was only first recorded by Yuri Kondratyuk (1897–1942), a Russian space scientist of the early twentieth century.[43]

Also innovative is the idea of creating an artificial habitat on a new world. After his arrival on Venus, Hope sets up an operating base stocked with supplies that is described as part "tent" and part "castle." Again, the idea of a "tent" to house the first Earth expedition to the Moon was only developed much later in the next century by the British Interplanetary Society.[44]

In terms of the science fiction genre, an intriguing plot device explicitly introduced by The Inhabitant is an awareness of possible regions in space through which passage would disable a spaceship. Hence the mention of the perils suffered by the *Star Climber* and its crew from a corrosive "Magellan cloud" that, instead of being located at the boundary of the Milky Way, is mistakenly found between Earth and Venus. Dangerous gas clouds in space have since become a staple of more recent science fiction, notably the original *Star Trek*'s second season episode "Obsession" (1967).

In terms of other original science fiction narrative devices, *The Great Romance* may also be the first story in which a person intentionally travels into the future via induced suspended animation rather than through an extended sleep; no earlier instance is mentioned by Bleiler in his history of the early years of science fiction.[45] Unlike Hope's sleep, West's stasis in *Looking Backward* was unintentional,

Introduction

as was Graham's in H. G. Wells's *The Sleeper Wakes* (1899). Furthermore, unlike other earlier suspended animation stories that "gloss over the scientific means by which suspended animation might be achieved,"[46] Hope, who is himself a renowned scientist of his own time, deliberately takes a potion concocted by his best friend, "John Malcolm Weir, the greatest chemist of his day" (1.50).

The Great Romance is not just innovative scientifically. An element additionally worth mentioning—which if not unique to nineteenth-century science fiction and utopianism is interesting in its own right—is the future relationship between the sexes. The society described in *The Great Romance* is a free-love society where "law and ceremony and promise are hardly needed" (1.26). Physical sexuality also looks to play a part in the relationship between Hope and Edith Weir: "It was with us, then, like Dante's lovers, when they ceased to read of the loves of Launcelot [*sic*] and the Queen" (1.26). As Hope meets Edith for the very first time at the beginning of volume 1, he admits to having experienced numerous sexual partners: "I was (that is before I slept) about fifty-six years old. I had known women in every form and phase. In my other life I had lived twelve years with one whose features I yet recall" (1.12). As he embarks for Venus he also appears to allude to his physical relationship with Edith, remembering "the happy hours" when they "drained to its dregs the cup of pleasure" (1.29).

While there appears to be a relatively liberal attitude expressed toward sexuality in *The Great Romance*, this does not imply that late-Victorian chauvinism had been done away with altogether, for the eventual expedition that goes to Venus is an entirely male one. Nowhere does the text even consider the possibility that some of the female characters in the story might accompany the first voyage, likely due to the potential dangers involved in such a long trip. Only once a safe route to Venus has been secured and the planet thoroughly explored can women perhaps follow. As such this twenty-second-century all-male trip to Venus is reminiscent of both eighteenth-century maritime voyages of exploration that consisted entirely of male crew members (with one exception), and of the early years of the modern American space program that, according to John Glenn, turned down female astronaut candidates only because of the nature of the country's social order.[47] Similarly, just after Hope wakes up and learns of the development of telepathy, he receives a warning from Weir: on account of his less-attractive countenance vis-à-vis the more beautiful citizens of the twenty-second century, when Hope reads thoughts he "will suffer most from women" since "their minds are less controllable than man's" (1.8). The Inhabitant, therefore, appears to be reaffirming the more traditional Victorian stereotypes that associated womanhood with physical and psychological weakness.

Although "Victorians were not in the habit of discussing . . . their sexual behaviour," the interest in sexuality expressed in *The Great Romance* is carried over to volume 2 and Hope's encounter with the Venuses.[48] Not only does Hope describe the alien couple whom he meets as nonchalantly engaging in a kind of sexual foreplay in his presence, he even appears to have begun pondering the consequences of cross-species miscegenation well before his first encounter with the aliens: "how our thoughts wondered over the intellectual union which might arise, should two such experiences join their pleasures, their results" (1.56). On the eve of departure for Venus the three astronauts also enjoy some comic banter about the potential offspring that might result from Moxton's and Hope's sexual encounters with a fantasy "Venusian," whom they imagine to be something of a "fish-like maiden" (1.36).

Such willingness by a late nineteenth-century New Zealand author to consider an intellectual and physical partnership with a distinctly alien life-form is worthy of note for two reasons: First, the earliest time that such a cross-species relationship in science fiction was considered had been thought to occur as late as 1925, when French author J. H. Rosny describes a love affair between a human and a six-eyed tripedal Martian in *The Navigators of Infinity*.[49] Second, such a relationship in *The Great Romance* might be indicative of the sexual interaction and intermarriage that occurred in colonial New Zealand

Introduction

between the Pakeha and Maori (if one assumes that the aliens are a substitute, whether consciously or not, for the Maori). Such mixing appears to have been tolerated officially by both peoples and would seem to make New Zealand's colonial attitudes toward the Maori rather unique in terms of ethnic relations, especially when compared with the experience of other indigenous groups of the British Empire during the nineteenth century. As Sorrenson suggests, "such marriages ... do not appear to have caused much Pakeha male jealousy; certainly there was no attempt to legislate them out of existence, as happened in Britain's African colonies."[50]

THE DEPICTION OF ALIENS

Adam Roberts writes, "It is not surprising that science fiction, a genre devoted to the encounter with difference, should have so often dramatized the various encounters of racial difference."[51] In *The Great Romance* the issue of interspecific relationships raises what is quite possibly one of the novel's most interesting developments, at least from a postcolonial perspective, namely, the creation of physiologically and psychologically believable extraterrestrials.

The Great Romance is certainly not the first work to develop the concept of life existing elsewhere in the universe. As early as the second century AD the Greek writer Lucian of Samosata had been peopling the Moon and other heavenly bodies with strange races, including half-human female-grapevines out of whose fingertips grew bunches of fully ripened grapes. Most of his creatures, however, fitted "more into supernatural fiction than ancestral science-fiction."[52] As such they were intended for didactic or satiric purposes, rather like the talking animals in Aesopian fantasy or Jonathan Swift's protoscience fictional Houyhnhnms in *Gulliver's Travels* (1726). The latter, with their emphasis on reason and ignorance of the human (or "Yahoo") emotions of love or sorrow, were depicted by Swift as living on a different metaphysical level from humankind. As such they do not seem to represent a convincing alien culture, although they may have functioned as a possible Enlightenment equivalent to *Star Trek*'s ultra-logical Vulcans.

Nor were the ancient Greeks the only civilization to develop this concept of *aperoi kosmoi*, an infinity of worlds. Non-European peoples such as the Chumash of California or the Pitdjandjara of western Australia had also evolved a concept of pluralism, a theory which by the early modern age had become fashionable in European circles as well. Among pluralism's eminent Western admirers are some of the greatest philosophical and scientific minds of the era, including Giordano Bruno, Galileo Galilei, René Descartes, John Locke, Alexander Pope, Thomas Paine, Benjamin Franklin, and Immanuel Kant. Pluralism received further attention in 1836 during what became known as the "Great Moon Hoax," when the owner of the *New York Sun* newspaper, in a successful bid to improve circulation, deliberately misinformed the public about the discovery of life on the Moon.[53]

However, those later nineteenth-century science fiction authors who built on these philosophical and scientific underpinnings and went on to develop a conception of intelligent alien beings, such as the "Martials" in *Across the Zodiac*, tended to restrict their descriptions to a type of humanoid that was biologically similar to humankind. John Pierce suggests that "until *The War of the Worlds*, interplanetary fiction had typically peopled other worlds with beings little different from ourselves."[54] The Martials in Greg's story, for example, are essentially shorter and weaker human beings. (The exception to this rule appears to be the sentient plants in the works of the French writer Camille Flammarion, namely *Real and Imaginary Worlds* [1864] and *Lumen* [1887].) According to Pierce this tendency was for plot reasons having to do either with a need to develop a human-alien romantic interest (in the works of Edgar Rice Burroughs) or a malevolent bug-eyed monster threat (in H. G. Wells). Pierce thus feels that, "for the most part, the story of aliens in science fiction before 1934 is one of missed opportunities."[55] Yet the Venuses in volume 2 of *The Great Romance* are a visibly more distinct species from *Homo sapiens*: "There before me in the uncertain distance some thing with two colourless insect-like wings stood stiffly up.... Strange beings! how shall I describe them? with no likeness to humanity except that they stood on two legs; with arms, yet not arms; faces human, yet how unlike! ... with soft eyes ... their fine bodies covered with a down—neither of bird nor animal—soft and dark, and their heavy, lithe limbs, such as might have developed from that earliest of prehistoric elephant" (2.71).

The two Venuses whom Hope encounters—a male and a smaller female, whose wings call to mind the bat wings of the *New York Sun*'s Moon beings—are also given a good deal of basic personal development. Furthermore, attempts are made to portray the Venuses with a realistic xenobiological characterization. For instance, when the two races first meet, hand gestures are required to initiate a greeting since the aliens do not speak English. These communication difficulties are a radical step forward from the talking animals in Aesopian fantasy. Likewise, more recent science fiction tended to ignore the problems of both spoken and nonverbal communication until the post–World War II period.[56] At first the smaller female alien even shrinks back with fear when Hope approaches to initiate a dialogue between their two peoples. Nonetheless, first contact between the Terran and Venusian species in *The Great Romance* appears, as Hope describes, particularly successful:

> Strange sounds they made; the huge limb [of the male alien] descended; it touched my hands with a soft motion; then I stroked that extended arm; and ... became emboldened and took the quaint ending of that limb in my hand, and shook it as I would a friend's hand. Then what was the laughter of the planet broke in motion over their faces.... It swept away my dread ... I went still nearer—I put an arm on each and laid my face against the face of the smaller one. (2.71)

The description of Hope and the aliens initiating physical touch and establishing mutual confidence includes a Maori-like hongi greeting when the two beings lay their faces against one another in a way similar to the rubbing of noses. Afterward they exchange gifts which, coupled with their greetings, are reminiscent of earlier eighteenth-century reactions by the Maori tribes of New Zealand to the crew of Capt. James Cook's *Endeavour*. Horeta Te Taniwha, a small child when the *Endeavour* first visited New Zealand's Whitianga harbor in November 1769, recalled in his memoirs how the women and children of the tribe at first ran away from the European "goblins" out of fright, but then, as they gained confidence, "came back one by one . . . [and] stroked their garments."[57] Similarly, the crew of Cook's *Endeavour* often presented visiting chiefs with gifts of linen or nails that they imagined would be valued by these visiting dignitaries.[58] *The Great Romance* is not the only science fiction work to incorporate indigenous customs into its narrative. One of the more recent examples is the adoption of a Sioux battle cry by *Star Trek*'s Klingons: "Today is a good day to die!"[59] Nevertheless, this adoption of Maori customs in the novella does make a postcolonial reading of the text particularly rewarding.

Aside from these seemingly naturalistic encounters that imitate British imperial contact experiences, the alien couple in *The Great Romance* also have their own particular belief system and complex code of social behavior, which suggests that The Inhabitant intended them to be more than one-dimensional personalities. While later agreeing to act as Hope's guides to the planet Venus, they first demand a kind of "solemn covenant" from Hope that he will never disclose the whereabouts of the other Venuses (2.95). As Hope presumes this to be an oath of secrecy he vows in reply that, "wherever your native home may be I will always hold it as a sacred thing" (2.95). Furthermore, once a friendship is established between Hope and the Venuses, the aliens continue to follow their own greeting customs even though Hope shakes their hands in his own tradition: "The Venuses would insist on going through their code of salutation—their long right arms would curl around Hope, then the smaller left arm would stroke in a soft, methodical manner" (2.94). Such a practice would seem to reflect both indigenous accommodation and a Venusian persistence to maintain their identity in the wake of a foreign presence. As such this behavior is very much in keeping with visual depictions of nineteenth- and twentieth-century Maori leaders, as demonstrated in L. C. Mitchell's painting *Reconstruction of the Signing of the Treaty of Waitangi* (1840) or the Tanner brothers' series of photographic images of prominent Maoris, such as Paora Tuhaere and Hori Ngakapa (1900), whereby beautiful ornamental cloaks, facial moko (tattoo) patterns, greenstone jewelry, and traditional cultural practices such as the haka were all emphasized as a conscious means of empowerment.

Before Hope's two Earth companions, Moxton and Weir, begin their return journey home from Venus, they "collected fruits, flowers, and the smaller animals, to be taken back" (2.66). Such an accumulation resembles modern expeditions to the Moon that returned with assorted bits of cosmic debris for analysis back home. Strikingly enough, such actions are also reminiscent of the missions of naturalists Joseph Banks and Daniel Solander, who accompanied Cook's journey to the South Pacific and whose aim was to collect rock, soil, and animal and insect samples of the places they visited during their long voyage of discovery (and, coincidentally, to observe the astronomical transit of none other than the planet Venus). As Banks is quoted saying, "No people ever went to sea better fitted out for the purpose of Natural History. . . . they have all sorts of machines for catching and preserving insects; all kinds of nets, trawls, drags and hooks for coral fishing."[60]

Despite reading like a safari adventure at times, with its descriptions of various "huge lion-like animals," tigers, fish, and strange landscapes, The Inhabitant's depiction of the planet appears to represent a believable alien-world creation. Likewise, the actions of his characters (both human and alien) appear realistic. Nevertheless, it should also be noted that Venus's landscape is more often than not merely an exotic variant of the Earth's and not so different from descriptions of foreign climes evident in other contemporary travelers' tales.

What underlines the uniqueness of the work, however, is the fact that on occasion the author appears sympathetic to these aliens. As early as volume 1, before contact has been made with the Venuses, Hope concludes that if alien life does exist on the planet then Earth colonists will just have to find another world to develop: "We must seek another planet—for earth's over-crowded happiness" (1.43). Similarly, the Venuses are described as having a degree of mental ability: "There was intelligence, knowledge, in every line of their features" (2.71). They are also depicted as being high up on the evolutionary scale: "These were not savages, and how far removed from animals" (2.72).

Discussing contact experiences in science fiction, John Pierce states that Florence Carpenter Dieudonné, in her work *Rondah; or, Thirty-Three Years in a Star* (1887), is "ahead of her time ... in defending the rights of aliens."[61] Likewise, Kingsley Amis states that sympathetic attitudes toward alien species (such as native peoples) were developed in American science fiction no earlier than the middle of the twentieth century.[62] The unwillingness by early science fiction authors to imagine friendly alien beings may in part be due to the influence of H. G. Wells and Darwinian concepts about the survival of the fittest. Science fiction authors may well have imagined most aliens as threatening since evolutionary philosophy seemed to turn them into natural competitors of humankind.[63] Certainly early anti-alien feelings would have reflected some of the negative racial stereotypes evident in numerous late nineteenth- and early twentieth-century Euro-American narratives, which depicted indigenous peoples as having subhuman, lazy, or dangerous personalities. Matabele warriors in South Africa, for example, were sometimes described as "daemons," while Australian Aborigines were often accused of cannibalism.[64]

Such racist perspectives are also in evidence in a great many of the utopian novels of this period, with "pigmentopias" to be found in works advocating all kinds of supposedly ideal political persuasions, whether they be anarchist, capitalist, or socialist.[65] According to Patrick Parrinder, Butler's *Erewhon* (1872) should in fact be read as "a major work in the eugenic utopian tradition," with ugly, sick, and dark-skinned peoples being excluded from its so-called perfect society.[66]

While the empathy evidenced for the Venuses in *The Great Romance* would appear to put the work ahead of its time in relation to the science fiction and utopian genres, such attitudes mirror the more favorable history of relations between Pakehas and Maoris—one that dramatically contrasted with the contact histories of European colonization in the Americas and Australia, many of whose indigenous peoples were displaced or eradicated during the settlement process.[67] As such the more positive images of the Venuses could reflect a Pakeha belief that the Maori demonstrated "a rare capacity for civilisation" and thus fitting the stereotype of the "noble savage."[68] According to Salmond this contributed to European perceptions of the Maori "as an innocent, happy child of Nature, free of the corruptions of 'civilised' society, the Utopian inheritor of the biblical Garden of Eden."[69] Not surprisingly, Hope refers to Venus as Eden and himself as "Adam" (2.75).

In British intellectual circles since the time of Edward Gibbon and Thomas Babington Macaulay, the Maori had historically held a privileged position as the cultural inheritors of the empire's *mission civilisatrice*. They were seen as the historical equivalent to the Gauls of France upon the collapse of the Roman Empire and as preservers of classical culture and knowledge. Such a romantic image, as far as the Maori-British "special relationship" is concerned, was most famously encapsulated in Gustave Doré's painting *The New Zealander* (1872) created for the publication *London: A Pilgrimage*, which depicted a solitary Maori figure contemplating the ruins of a future London.[70]

ORIENTALIZING THE VENUSES

Despite the initial sympathy for the aliens that makes the two novellas so different from conventional science fiction, the existence of a number of paternalistic elements toward the Venuses cannot be ignored. These paternalistic attitudes mirror late nineteenth-century cultural attitudes of racial superiority toward native peoples and simultaneously expose a more ambiguous and complex attitude to racial categorizing. Although in volume 1 Hope states that colonization would not proceed should there be life on Venus, the idea is quickly forgotten by volume 2, for even after Hope has befriended the Venuses he still has grand plans for the alien world: "They had come to find a future home for the growing millions of their native earth, and here all around the tropical zone was a region fitted with everything necessary" (2.88). This imperialistic chauvinism is also visible in the fact that Hope has his own version of a frontier fort where he can retreat if attacked, his "little castle" with its "formidable ... powers of defence" (2.63). Furthermore, the spaceship in which the three companions travel to Venus is described as being very well defended: "Our offensive powers were certainly enormous. A cannon or mortar was almost built into the vessel, yet swivel-working with patent discharge, so that with its mouth in space it could pour forth such an incessant stream of fierce projectiles as might frighten the boldest adversary" (1.35).

The inclusion of a well-defended spaceship and fortified retreat mirrors both the defensive precautions taken onboard Captain Cook's *Endeavour*, which included a complement of marines and weapons, and the frontier forts of the American West. As a further safeguard Hope carries a revolver, and even after befriending the alien couple he brings a still more powerful revolver—just to be on the safe side. At this same time, Hope does admit to a feeling of guilt for bringing this weapon along: "Afterwards I thought almost with shame at my doubts concerning my gentle companions" (2.72).

Such lingering uncertainties on the part of Hope toward his newfound alien friends might also reflect prevailing Pakeha anxieties in the wake of the New Zealand Wars. These frontier conflicts saw certain Maori tribes going to war with both the settler government and other Maori tribes over issues such as land and mana (authority). Although these wars had ended by the early 1870s, an armed constabulary remained garrisoned in the North Island of the colony until 1885, and in the early 1880s peaceful Maori protests against the government's confiscation of native lands—as payment and punishment for enemy Maori tribes supporting the war effort—were conducted in the Taranaki District by leaders such as Te Whiti. As Sorrenson notes, "A raw military edge to race relations thus persisted until the early twentieth century."[71] Nor was New Zealand the only colony in which indigenous tribes, although allied to the British, were still treated with some suspicion. In South Africa indigenous auxiliaries remained underarmed with inferior weapons, despite the fact that Zulu warriors were employed in the service of the empire to help quell an 1878 insurrection by fellow Zulus. These supplementary precautions were still not enough to offset the outrage expressed by elements in that country toward the arming of black groups, especially when the white population was outnumbered ten to one.[72] All in all, "colonial rule was frequently haunted by a sense of insecurity," a factor that *The Great Romance* exploits.[73]

A number of other acts that Hope undertakes could be interpreted as examples of imperial conceit as well. Soon after contact with the Venuses, Hope begins naming them. What is more, he chooses the classical appellations of Philomenia [*sic*] and Hyperion, and in so doing automatically appropriates the legacy of the Greco-Roman heritage and all its resonances of civilized authority. This was a favorite tactic of late nineteenth-century empire propagandists. According to Jan Nederveen Pieterse, "in the Protestant countries ... classicism was the uniform of civilization."[74] Such a naming process is in fact very similar to the way Robinson Crusoe names his companion Friday, although Hope does recognize that "he would learn their own names as soon as he could master their most strange speech" (2.88).

Additionally, Hope tends to view the Venuses, despite their intelligence, as "children" (2.72) whose minds "had little that was superior to humanity. . . . of that great body of thought which has arisen from our mechanical and omnivorous propensities, they knew nothing" (2.78). The association of the indigene with the childlike helped to foster an impression that native peoples were primitive and inferior and in need of education which consequently was seen to necessitate and justify white intervention and control, as was the case in Australia when white officials viewed Aborigines as "a race of humanity who had not quite grown up."[75] Those images of arrested indigenous development were further reinforced by the perceived low level of material culture achieved by these groups. Such interpretations were a carryover from Enlightenment thinkers such as David Hume who assumed that since Africans had not apparently produced anything of "substantial" material significance, blacks were "naturally inferior to whites."[76]

Such cultural assumptions are evident in *The Great Romance*, witnessed by Hope's dismissal of the Venuses' little boat as "rude" and his portrayal of their primitive-looking home: "[Their] hut or nest appeared built on piles—out in the water, covered with grass and boughs, and only to be approached by coming along a row of stilt-like piles driven between it and the land" (2.77). Hope's racial superiority, and by implication the Venuses' own inferiority, is also made manifest in volume 2 when Hope begins to "civilize" them. He shows them the benefits of fire and teaches them to cook the local fish, in the process commenting that they will soon be "as completely civilised in these respects as the inhabitants of the earth" (2.78). The apparent sexual behavior of the Venuses toward one another (as discussed above) could have indicated to a Victorian audience a relatively uncivilized manner. It was certainly the case that images of naked indigenous peoples in the photography of the time became the subject of severe missionary criticism and served as an indicator of the supposed deprived spiritual state of the people concerned. Nevertheless, a curiosity about the sexual practices of different peoples might have also reflected an interest in exotic eroticism that bordered on the pornographic and closely resembled European fantasies of the harem in Orientalist description.

One of the more obvious aspects of *The Great Romance* indicating imperial attitudes of late-colonial New Zealand society concerns the discussions of race and eugenics that recur again and again in much of the narrative, particularly in volume 1. As soon as Hope wakes up he is told that humanity has advanced beyond measure, borne out by the physical strength and beauty of the planet's inhabitants; the descriptions of these advanced humans as "holy" and of "perfection" (1.9); the advent of telekinesis (implying superhuman capabilities); and the fact that telepathy has done away with crime on most of the planet, at least "among the higher races" (1.9). The latter suggests that there are pockets on Earth where such mental and physiological advances have yet to be realized, something that is later admitted by Edith Weir when she tells Hope that "the Hottentot, the degraded Negro, and the great border lands of peoples" are "not yet incorporated in the kingdom of thought" (1.27). Edith also tells Hope, however, that such nations are in decline and that the peoples living there, while presently outnumbered ten to one, will soon be outnumbered one hundred to one (1.27).

Edith's emphasis on population numbers could reflect the doomed race theory that was contemporary to the Victorian era and envisioned nonwhite indigenous groups, such as the Aboriginal Australians, Native Americans, and Maori, as slowly dying out as a result of a Darwinian-inspired belief in the evolutionary process of natural selection. By 1891 the Maori population in New Zealand had decreased to about 7 percent of the colony's total population, while by contrast the number of Pakehas was still on the increase.[77] By 1890 the European population of the islands had exceeded that of the indigenous people by a ratio of ten to one, a figure not too far removed from the one given by Edith.[78] To some nineteenth-century observers, therefore, it looked as though the Maori would soon go the way of their Tasmanian cousins across the sea, a concern that *The Great Romance* may well have reflected. Consequently, Hope's willingness to consider miscegenation with the aliens might be indicative of attempts by some Pakeha to "save" the Maori through amalgamation with white New Zealanders.

Yet Edith's emphasis on the population ratio between the "lower" and "higher races" might also have mirrored the even darker "War of the Races" topos that emerged in xenophobic Anglo-American literature, such as in M. P. Shiel's *The Yellow Danger* (1898) or Jack London's "The Unparalleled Invasion" (1910), both of which exposed a sense of insecurity about foreign invasion by nonwhite groups. Consequently, the emphasis on declining numbers of nonwhites in *The Great Romance* may have been intended to assuage such white anxieties.

These sorts of hierarchal anxieties are not only evident between white and black peoples in *The Great Romance*; there are disparities within the ranks of the "advanced" white population of the future as well. Edith Weir's father, when discussing Hope's desire to travel to Venus in volume 1, criticizes his decision on the basis that such a voyage would be dangerous; he states that other less valuable persons could take his place: "Well, Hope, you are a fool.... When there are hundreds of useless, dull-brained animals whose loss would be no detriment to anything, you must go" (1.30). It appears that classlike disparities, as well as racial ones, are still integral to the vision of society in the twenty-second century.

COLONIZING VENUS

One apocryphal story of the late 1960s recounted that when NASA astronauts were training in the Arizona desert as part of their preparations for a Moon landing, they came across an elderly Navajo shepherd and asked him if he had any messages for the inhabitants of the Moon. The shepherd apparently replied, "Be careful. They will steal your land."[79] The shepherd's comment raises what is another interesting aspect of *The Great Romance*, that of the colonization of Venus by humankind. John Clute and Peter Nicholls, in *The Encyclopedia of Science Fiction*, point out that while H. G. Wells was one of the earliest science fiction writers to borrow from the example of British colonial history for his famous Martian invasion of Earth in *The War of the Worlds* (1898), Wells never envisioned the converse settlement

Introduction

of Mars by humankind.[80] Moreover, Clute and Nicholls conclude that "later writers of Scientific Romance were also completely uninterested in the conquest of space," although Lucian's second century work, *True History*, did recount the story of an attempt by peoples of the Moon to colonize the Sun.[81] Thus, not only does *The Great Romance* appear to be one of the first science fiction works to seriously handle the subject of the colonization of space (a theme in science fiction that, like alien creatures, has since become a staple of the modern genre), the nonchalant treatment of the colonization of Venus by the earthlings additionally serves to underline the imperialistic metanarrative that runs through much of the work.

Very early in volume 1 the issue of the colonization of space is raised when Hope, after seeing the fantastic technological advances of the future and the biological superiority of Earth's inhabitants, wonders if the power behind creation deliberately "left the rest of the solar system for our increase, for the increase of those godlike moving beings" (1.12). Halfway through the first volume substantial plans are already afoot for the human settlement of Venus, even before it has been thoroughly explored or it can be determined if alien life already exists on the planet (not to mention whether or not its inhabitants would welcome such an intrusion): "Should we reach Venus, I had intended to stay while Moxton and Weir returned. ... Then Weir would lead the second voyage, and were it practicable Edith and Lucy Moxton would come with others. The boats for the second voyage now were far advanced" (1.33).

The emphasis upon an armada of spaceships is worthy of further comment. Preparing numerous vessels to transport colonists had historical precedents, such as when Capt. Arthur Phillip's First Fleet landed in New South Wales (minus the convict element). But this is the first space fleet in the history of science fiction. As such it predates the 1898 novel *Edison's Conquest of Mars*, whose author, Garrett P. Serviss, is reputed to have "created the first-ever scenes of massed fleets of interplanetary spaceships."[82]

During the process of befriending the alien couple, Hope concludes that the ecology of the planet must be solely geared toward supporting an isolated and nomadic hunter-gatherer existence, as large Venus settlements do not seem to exist. "If they lived without tillage on the fruits of ground," Hope considers, "they must need be few in number, and live far apart" (2.77). Yet even after contact with the Venuses and the realization that the planet's environment is fragile and only suited to the Venuses' particular mode of life, Hope still dreams of other humans following in his footsteps: "Here, too, should reign the works of man, and this planet should teem with human pleasure" (2.87). It is not surprising, then, that Hope initially found it difficult to induce the aliens to show him the way to the rest of their people.

One of the reasons for Earth's attempted colonization of Venus in *The Great Romance*, apart from the need to relieve the Earth of its growing population, is a desire to further improve upon the human condition and ensure that the human race does not go into decline. Such a motive is touched upon by Alfred Malcolm Weir, the brother of Edith Weir and also the first person to raise with Hope the issue of colonizing other planets: "We are dreaming now of other worlds—of Mars and Venus. Could we reach them and inhabit them life might again increase, I don't think we should feel degraded, at least for two or three hundred years" (1.9). Weir's comments express a late nineteenth-century British concern about race degeneration, epitomized by the birth of the motherhood movement, the growing popularity of eugenic ideas, calls for female emigrants to the colonies, and widespread anxiety over military and industrial decline in the wake of German, American, and Japanese rivalry. Such anxieties might account for the repeated references to elixirs of immortality as a means for humanity to avoid death and decline.

Considering the theme of colonization in *The Great Romance*, it is not a stretch of the imagination to read the work as a promotional piece encouraging emigration. As Clute and Nicholls point out, because of New Zealand's distance from Old World centers of power, the colony became "a convenient setting for moral and Utopian tales," a factor that explains why propagandists for New Zealand, such as Richard Wedderspoon in *The Dominion of New Zealand* (1927), all too often reiterated it in their promotional literature.[83] The emphasis on friendly aliens may even be part of a booster strategy intended to assure European readers concerned about rebellious Maori in the post-1860s New Zealand Wars climate. It was certainly the case that as late as the 1920s, New Zealand promoters were attempting to show that the country was not just a "half-developed land peopled chiefly by copper-coloured natives and a few white settlers," while its filmmakers, in motion pictures such as *The Adventures of Algy* (1925), poked fun at comical Englishmen arriving by steamship in Auckland harbor armed with guns to ward off Maori attacks.[84]

The actual choice of the planet Venus for human settlement, as opposed to the Moon or Mars, also underscores the colonialist promotional theme. Although early on in volume 1 Venus is decided upon as a destination because of its atmosphere, it may actually have more to do with boosting strong imperialistic elements within the text. Consider that in ancient Italian mythology Venus was a minor deity identified with the spring and vegetation and that classical female imagery associated with Venus was often employed by European maritime powers to signify land as a resource to be penetrated and exploited. When Amerigo Vespucci, for instance, described the continent of America, he imagined it as a benevolent and fertile female figure who, with her cornucopia, offered untold wealth and riches to all.[85] Such classical associations of land with femininity would not have been lost on The Inhabitant. Throughout the text he demonstrates his classical education in choosing Latin names for the Venuses and making references to various Renaissance works of literature. The choice of the name Philomena ("beloved") for the female alien, not to mention Venus's later Roman association with Aphrodite as the goddess of love, might additionally allude to the protagonist's contemplation of sexual relations across species lines. It was certainly the case that descriptions of early planetary tours to Venus, such as in Emanuel Swedenborg's *The Earths in our Solar*

System (1758), "were influenced by the planet's long-time association with the goddess of love."[86]

It has been suggested that nineteenth-century science fiction remained uncommitted to the colonization of other planets on account of "a sense of shame about the methods employed in colonizing terrestrial lands."[87] As early as 1818 even the monster in Mary Shelley's *Frankenstein* is critical of the results of colonization: "I heard of the discovery of the American hemisphere and wept with Safie over the hapless fate of its original inhabitants."[88] Likewise, when distinct alien beings were eventually introduced into early twentieth-century science fiction, they were usually depicted as bug-eyed monsters. *The Great Romance*, therefore, would seem to run counter to this general trend in science fiction by emphasizing both the human settlement of Venus and a unique vision of friendly aliens who are physically (and to some extent culturally) distinct from humanity. This positive depiction of alienness in the work also gives *The Great Romance* an added importance at a theoretical level. It goes some way toward substantiating critical responses in postcolonial literature to Edward Said's *Orientalism*, and demonstrates that western representations of the Other are often far more complex and ambiguous than Said's early work assumed. As John McLeod points out, "Cross-currents of 'Orientalist' or 'counter-Orientalist' thinking can exist simultaneously within a single text."[89]

Said's work, first published in 1978, was essentially a study of how North African and Middle Eastern peoples were portrayed in western colonial representations that sought to legitimize European rule and domination as, among other things, backward, strange, degenerate, and feminine. One early critical response to Said's work, Dennis Porter's "Orientalism and Its Problems" (1983), suggested that Said's critique was ahistorical in that it made sweeping generalizations about two thousand years of history without examining individual moments in time. Porter argued that "even the most seemingly Orientalist text can include within itself moments when Orientalist assumptions come up against alternative views that throw their authority into question."[90] John MacKenzie, in his *Orientalism: History, Theory and the Arts* (1995), expanded on Porter's criticism and argued that "western artists have approached the Orient at various moments with perfectly honourable intentions and 'genuine respect.'"[91] In a similar vein Nicholas Thomas has suggested, this time with regard to representations of the colonized in anthropology and traveler narratives, that colonial discourse should not be approached only "as a global and transhistorical logic of denigration."[92]

An initial examination of the more optimistic depiction of the Venuses in *The Great Romance* would appear to corroborate much of what Porter, MacKenzie, and Thomas state. First, although the alien couple indulges in foreplay at a time in history and literature when overt sexuality was envisioned as a sign of immorality and lack of control, The Inhabitant does also describe the future utopian earth as a free-love community and Hope does more than hint at having had a number of relationships with women outside of marriage. So it is not just the aliens who indulge in overt sexual behavior. Second, despite the two aliens being depicted as primitive childlike figures, they are not described as lazy, violent, or untrustworthy. Indeed, Hope chastises himself for his very own lack of trust in them. Additionally, the aliens are not stereotyped superficially as one-dimensional characters. Rather, the author of the work has made a genuine attempt to portray them as believable and friendly beings whose nonhuman appearance, customs, language, and agency depict them in a positive light. This optimistic treatment of the colonized remains a far cry from More's *Utopia* (1516), where King Utopos had all the indigenes ethnically cleansed from his "ideal" state.

In his critique of Said's work, Mackenzie also pointed out that *Orientalism* "failed to make any distinction between 'high art' and popular culture," suggesting, like Porter, that Said should have been wary of generalizations.[93] The fact that a possible site of counter-hegemonic resistance comes from a work of science fiction—a genre dismissed by some as not "proper" literature and unworthy of serious study—would seem at first glance to substantiate much of Mackenzie's critical approach.

Despite this early optimism, there is also a darker side to The

Inhabitant's depiction of a golden future for the human race among the Venuses, one that shows that even sympathetic representations of the Other are not always free from latent Orientalist assumptions. First, not all Earth peoples are yet able to share in The Inhabitant's idealized vision of the shape of things to come, as black Africans (among other groups) are explicitly excluded. Second, although Hope feigns sympathy for the Venuses, it is only too clear where his real sympathies lie, namely, with the racially and culturally superior human race searching for lebensraum among the stars. And, third, if English-speaking science fiction authors were indeed critical of the colonization of other planets on account of Britain's imperial legacy, then the introduction of a cooperative, welcoming, and allied alien species in *The Great Romance* might simply function as a convenient ruse to help counteract any feelings of remorse or guilt. Certainly the more subtle theme of cooperative locals was also one means emphasized domestically by British authorities to help justify Britain's overlordship of Africa and the Pacific.[94]

Overall, the ambivalent attitudes expressed more often than not toward the Venuses and other nonwhite human groups by characters such as Edith and Hope, when compounded by the Orientalist-like descriptions of the Venuses as childlike or backward, the subtle use of science and reason to legitimize colonization, and the overt references to eugenics and race, further suggests that an imperial conceit runs throughout *The Great Romance*. If one deconstructs the story as an alternative ontological history of contact between the Maori and the British over the course of the nineteenth century, one that merely uses the alien-human story as a surrogate for this relationship, then it is not surprising that things still turned out the way they did despite the initial optimism for cooperation between these groups that followed in the wake of the signing of the 1840 Treaty of Waitangi. As John McLeod comments about the general results of such well-intentioned and benign colonialism, "the road to hell is often paved with good intentions."[95]

Addressing the criticism that Said overlooked the contradictory

Introduction

elements and multiple readings possible in some colonial writings, MacKenzie's emphasis on the need for a kind of Rankean-inspired historicist approach to each period that recognizes resistance to imperialist conceits, and the more unique contact history of the Pakehas and Maoris, the central colonialist assumptions about Orientalism, as far as *The Great Romance* is concerned, still appear to remain valid, albeit in a muted form.

CONCLUSION

The Great Romance stands out from contemporary science fiction works in a number of ways, including its possible influence on Bellamy and its radical position both in the writing of science fiction and its vision of the future of space exploration. It is not, therefore, the primitive or absurd novel that is, in places, dismissed by the writer of that 1882 review in *Otago Daily Times*. Yet, leaving aside the still-unproved Bellamy link as well as its scientific acumen, the work remains interesting as a kind of cultural barometer. Like much other science fiction, it can be used as an alternative means for analyzing popular perceptions of a specific historical period, in much the same way that more modern science fiction works—such as the original film *Invasion of the Body Snatchers* (Siegel, 1956) or the old television series *Star Trek* (Roddenberry, 1966–69)—can be used to examine Cold War paranoia in the 1950s or a change in American opinion toward the Vietnam War in the late 1960s.

The Great Romance is also of interest from a literary point of view. Although there are holes and inconsistencies in the plot, some serious errors in the narrative structure, and the inclusion of a number of poems without any introduction, attribution of authorship, or indication of how they are intended to relate to the prose, the work still reads moderately well.[96] While the meaning can be unclear in places and, as Ray Hargreaves rightly points out, it "certainly cannot be claimed to be great New Zealand literature," the writing is not quite as dull and drawn out as a good deal of similar contemporaneous science fiction and utopian material.[97] We are saved, for example, from the long-winded lectures by Dr. Leete on the virtues of nationalization that can be found in Bellamy's *Looking Backward*. In places the text even borders on the lyrical, as witnessed by the description of Venus as seen from a meteor: "Overhead stretched an inky purple sky, pierced with pale points of light, little, faint white stars. The sun was hidden from them, and the planet they had left shone like a miniature moon—a pale crescent" (2.99).

The text's readability could, of course, be merely due to the fact that the entirety is only ninety-four pages in length. Nevertheless, considering that *The Great Romance* is so brief, the very fact that it contains such a substantial quantity of interesting material is itself testimony to the caliber of the vision behind the work. The concluding episode, focused on Hope's companions on the meteor and particularly Weir's fall off the face of the planetoid is gripping and visionary, despite what *The Oxford Companion to New Zealand Literature* suggests. It is literally a cliff-hanging conclusion to the second volume.

In terms of plot, one interesting aspect related to telepathy that appears to make *The Great Romance* superior to *Looking Backward* is the logic of Hope's romantic relationship with Edith, especially when contrasted to the illogical nature of West's pairing with Bellamy's Edith. As pointed out by Parrinder, since the Boston of the year 2000 is an advanced eugenic society, how is it that Bellamy's Edith is able to fall in love with a backward and primitive visitor from the past yet attain the consent of her parents to do so?[98] Hope, on the other hand, is a much better candidate for a future utopian eugenic love interest. Although he is certainly older and more "ugly" than the potential suitors of Edith's own time, he is one of the most intelligent minds from his century, having "first started the mechanical world on this new track" (1.7) and has, according to the twenty-second-century Weir, the capacity to develop telepathy: "As soon as you become a little more accomplished in our language of thought you will read the laws of morals and manners in the mind of every one you converse with" (1.17).

Introduction

Some literary critics in New Zealand have made a number of generalizations concerning the late nineteenth- and early twentieth-century colonial cultural scene. Peter Gibbons once dismissed New Zealand's artistic output in this period as "the age of the cow-cockies" in contrast to Europe's "era of futuristic . . . art."[99] Similarly, Russell Brown has noted in a discussion about national identity in New Zealand that many former critics viewed the country's inhabitants as uninspiring and far too practical.[100] Yet, as the utopian and cutting-edge elements of *The Great Romance* indicate, perhaps New Zealand's cultural outlook was not necessarily always quite as backward or pragmatic as has been generally assumed, if it can be measured by a few works of science fiction. Vogel's *Anno Domini 2000* has been hailed by Roger Robinson as a particularly "percipient prophetic novel . . . [coming] nearer the mark than George Orwell's *1984* (1949) or most other futuristic imaginings," particularly with regard to its forward-thinking vision of female enfranchisement and political power.[101] Likewise, Samuel Butler's *Erewhon* "is generally regarded as ranking with More's *Utopia* and Swift's *Gulliver's Travels* as an iconic fiction of lasting importance."[102] New Zealand was also the site for the world's second earliest science fiction film. After France's Georges Méliès (1861–1938) produced *Voyage dans la Lune* in 1902, *A Message from Mars* came out in New Zealand in 1903.[103] The film, directed by Walter Franklyn Barrett (1873–1964), was based on a story written by the American Richard Ganthoney in 1899, for a theatrical production that had successfully toured the United Kingdom, the United States, and Australia. Gathoney's tale, loosely based on Dickens's *A Christmas Carol* (1843), recounted the story of a Martian sent to the Earth to prevent an individual's selfishness. Although the film has apparently not survived, what is significant about its production is that a semi-science fiction storyline was also New Zealand's first fiction film. Even perhaps more tellingly for a discussion of the relationship between the fantastic and New Zealand, the first mention in English of the term *robot* may have come from the pen of a New Zealand soldier writing about his experiences on the Western Front during World War I and not, as generally assumed, from the 1920 Czech play *R.U.R.*[104]

The Great Romance should now, at the very least, be acknowledged as a much more important work of New Zealand utopian and science fiction than heretofore recognized. As fiction it should also help to undermine a number of general assumptions regarding the so-called backwardness of the New Zealand cultural scene at the turn of the nineteenth century. Just as John Mackenzie's criticisms about the elitism of Said's approach in *Orientalism* helped to draw attention to competing counterhegemonic readings in western culture, a reevaluation of the science fiction and utopian tradition in New Zealand may throw new light on hitherto obscure quarters of the former colony's literary scene.

In terms of *The Great Romance*'s own future in the twenty-first century, what remains is to try and find volume 3, if it exists at all. Certainly the 1882 reviewer at the *Otago Daily Times* claimed "there is yet more to come," and the continuing references to ordered groups of alien maritime and land animals might suggest a future plot development. Perhaps most important, however, is the continued search for the identity of The Inhabitant, as he or she may hold the key to the text's unique place in the history of New Zealand's letters as well as its place among science fiction and utopian literature. It is hoped that this republication will go some way toward raising interest in that direction.

NOTES

1. The copy of volume 1 in the Alexander Turnbull Library is unique in having two title pages, one making Dunedin the place of publication, the other Ashburton. The Dunedin title page was printed at the *Otago Daily Times*, the Ashburton one at the *Guardian*. Since nearly all of the advertising is for Ashburton business firms, it seems likely that the Alexander Turnbull Library volume was published at Ashburton. Volume 2, however, was printed in Dunedin at the *Daily Times Office* and no other press is mentioned.

Introduction

2. Alkon, *Science Fiction Before 1900*, 107.
3. Bellamy's "To Whom This May Come" was originally published in the February 1889 issue of *Harper's* magazine and later enjoyed republication in his collection of short stories entitled *The Blindman's World and Other Stories* (1898), as well as H. Bruce Franklin's *Future Perfect* (1966) and Arthur O. Lewis's *American Utopias* (1971). It is now available in its entirety on the Internet.
4. Sorrenson, "Maori and Pakeha," 169.
5. Ashburton District Council, "Ashburton District Profile: Other Attractions," http://www.ashburtondc.govt.nz/district/district+profile.htm.
6. Bagnall, *Bibliography of New Zealand*, 1:520; and Sargent, *New Zealand Utopian Literature*, 6.
7. Information provided by the Hocken Library, reference PA 176/5.
8. Mann, "Science Fiction," 482.
9. Clute and Nicholls, *Encyclopedia of Science Fiction*, 869.
10. Alessio, *Science Fiction Studies* 20:305–40; Alessio, *Kōtare* 1:59–101; Alessio, *Kōtare* 2:48–79; Alessio, *Kōtare* 2:3–17; and Alessio, *ARIEL* 33:5–36.
11. Kirsten Thomlinson (former archivist at the Hocken Library, Dunedin), e-mail message to author, February 20, 2001.
12. Katherine Milburn (archivist at the Hocken Library, Dunedin), e-mail message to author, May 31, 2006.
13. Garry Tee, e-mail message to author, June 14, 2004.
14. Katherine Milburn (archivist at the Hocken Library, Dunedin), e-mail message to author, May 31, 2006.
15. Unsigned review of *The Great Romance*, by The Inhabitant, *Otago Daily Times* supplement, February 18, 1882, 1.
16. Bellamy, *Looking Backward*, 46.
17. Bellamy, *Looking Backward*, 43.
18. Fairburn, *Ideal Society*; and Fairburn, *New Zealand Journal of History* 20:3–21.
19. Alessio, *Foundation*, no. 91:36–54.
20. Paul Miller, "Bell, Col. George William," 51.
21. Lipow, *Authoritarian Socialism in America*, 23.
22. Alkon, *Science Fiction Before 1900*, 109.
23. Davis, *Utopia and the Ideal Society*, 37.
24. Clute and Nicholls, *Encyclopedia of Science Fiction*, 390.
25. Stone-Blackburn, *Science Fiction Studies*, 20:247.

26. Morgan, *Edward Bellamy*, 241.
27. Macnie, *The Diothas*, 58.
28. Pringle, *Ultimate Encyclopedia of Science Fiction*, 50.
29. Ordway, "Dreams of Space Travel," 35.
30. Ordway, "Dreams of Space Travel," 47.
31. Suvin, *Metamorphoses of Science Fiction*, 80.
32. Moskowitz, introduction to *Across the Zodiac*, 2.
33. Clute and Nicholls, *Encyclopedia of Science Fiction*, 517.
34. Baker, *Manned Space Flight*, 13.
35. Baker, *Manned Space Flight*, 14.
36. Baker, *Manned Space Flight*, 14.
37. Ron Miller, "The Spaceship As Icon," 68.
38. Winter, "Planning for Spaceflight," 107.
39. Richard A. Proctor, *Other Worlds than Ours* (1870), quoted in Hennessey, *Worlds Without End*, 80.
40. Hennessey, *Worlds Without End*, 60.
41. Hennessey, *Worlds Without End*, 80–93.
42. Baker, *Manned Space Flight*, 16; and Winter, "Planning for Spaceflight," 107.
43. Baker, *Manned Space Flight*, 14.
44. Baker, *Manned Space Flight*, 16.
45. Bleiler, *Science-Fiction*.
46. Clute and Nicholls, *Encyclopedia of Science Fiction*, 1189.
47. Bob Graham once insisted that he'd "prefer to send a monkey into space than a bunch of women." *Sunday Times Magazine*, November 15, 1998, 44.
48. Sorrenson, "Maori and Pakeha," 169.
49. Clute and Nicholls, *Encyclopedia of Science Fiction*, 15.
50. Sorrenson, "Maori and Pakeha," 192.
51. Roberts, *Science Fiction*, 118.
52. Bleiler, *Science-Fiction*, 455.
53. For a discussion of pluralism see Hennessey, *World Without End*.
54. Pierce, *Foundations of Science Fiction*, 93.
55. Pierce, *Themes of Science Fiction*, 2.
56. Clute and Nicholls, *Encyclopedia of Science Fiction*, 723, 751.
57. Salmond, *Two Worlds*, 87.
58. Salmond, *Two Worlds*, 162.

Introduction

59. Roberts, *Science Fiction*, 131.
60. Joseph Banks, *The Endeavour Journal of Joseph Banks 1768–1771*, ed. J. C. Beaglehole, 2 vols. (Sydney: Angus and Robertson, 1962), quoted in Salmond, 102.
61. Pierce, *Foundations of Science Fiction*, 59.
62. Amis, *New Maps of Hell*, 95.
63. Clute and Nicholls, *Encyclopedia of Science Fiction*, 16.
64. Alessio, *Journal of Imperial and Post-Colonial Historical Studies* 1:71–112.
65. For a discussion of "pigmentopia" see Alessio, *Journal of New Zealand Literature* 22:73–94. Brigitte Koenig, in a talk given at the 2006 Utopian Studies Society Conference, has pointed out that most U.S. anarchist utopias at the end of the nineteenth century were also racist at heart.
66. Parrinder, *Critical Survey* 17:6–21.
67. Such sympathetic attitudes toward alien beings might also reflect a growing interest in spiritualism as late nineteenth-century mediums were claiming to communicate with wise and friendly extraterrestrials. (Shaun Broadley, e-mail message to author, February 7, 2000.) Although The Inhabitant's link with spiritualism remains unproven, it was certainly not uncommon for New Zealanders such as Robert Stout (who went on to become prime minister) or other science fiction writers (e.g., Edward Bulwer-Lytton) to express a degree of interest in the practice.
68. Sorrenson, "Maori and Pakeha," 169.
69. Salmond, *Two Worlds*, 95.
70. Blanchard and Doré, *London*, 188.
71. Sorrenson, "Maori and Pakeha," 188.
72. Alessio, *Journal of Imperial and Post-Colonial Historical Studies* 1:71–112.
73. Thomas, *Colonialism's Culture*, 15.
74. Pieterse, *White on Black*, 19
75. McGregor, *Imagined Destinies*, 74.
76. Goldberg, *Racist Culture*, 31.
77. Sorrenson, "Maori and Pakeha," 192.
78. Sorrenson, "Maori and Pakeha," 168.
79. Tim Cornwell, "Two Tribes Go To War Over claims To Indian Territory," *Independent*, March 3, 1997, national edition.
80. Clute and Nicholls, *Encyclopedia of Science Fiction*, 244.
81. Clute and Nicholls, *Encyclopedia of Science Fiction*, 244. The one excep-

tion regarding early science fiction's avoidance of colonial themes, according to Clute and Nicholls, was Andrew Blair's *Annals of the Twenty-Ninth Century* (1874). Clute and Nicholls dismiss this, however, as a rather ponderous story of a protagonist's journey among the planets "whose inhabitants demonstrate various levels of spiritual perfection" (132).

82. Ron Miller, "The Spaceship As Icon," 55.
83. Clute and Nicholls, *Encyclopedia of Science Fiction*, 869.
84. Wedderspoon, *The Dominion of New Zealand*, 22.
85. Klarer, *Journal of American Studies* 27:5.
86. Clute and Nicholls, *Encyclopedia of Science Fiction*, 1274.
87. Clute and Nicholls, *Encyclopedia of Science Fiction*, 244.
88. Shelley, *Frankenstein*, 115.
89. McLeod, *Beginning Postcolonialism*, 51.
90. McLeod, *Beginning Postcolonialism*, 51.
91. Mackenzie, *Orientalism*, 60.
92. Thomas, *Colonialism's Culture*, 3.
93. Mackenzie, *Orientalism*, 14.
94. Alessio, *Journal of Imperial and Post-Colonial Historical Studies* 1:71–112.
95. McLeod, *Beginning Postcolonialism*, 48.
96. Examples of such errors abound: Telepathy is relatively important in volume 1 but appears to be forgotten in volume 2 when Weir and Moxton seem to speak directly to one another. There is a sudden change in the narrative structure from a first to third person narrator between chapters 16 and 17 of volume 2. There are no chapter titles in volume 1, but they appear in volume 2. The protagonist's middle name switches between Brenton, Bentford, and Bredford. There is no explanation why the Venuses have wings when they don't seem capable of flight. And initially during first contact Hope seems to see three Venuses, but the number reverts to two without explanation.
97. Ray Hargreaves, review of *The Great Romance*, by The Inhabitant, *Dunedin Star Weekender*, June 5, 1994, 19. There is also an unpublished version of this review shelved with *The Great Romance* (Pan 1881 INH 1143b) at the Alexander Turnbull Library in Wellington.
98. Parrinder, *Critical Survey* 17:8.
99. Gibbons, "The Climate of Opinion," 314.
100. McLauchlan, *New Zealand Books* 15:8.
101. Robinson, introduction to *Anno Domini 2000*, 11.

Introduction

102. Robinson, "Erewhon or Over the Range," 166.
103. *Australian Dictionary of Biography*, s.v. "Barrett, Walter Franklyn (1873-1964)" (by Martha Rutledge), http://www.adb.online.anu.edu.au/biogs/A070195b.htm.
104. Belich, *Paradise Reforged*, 105. Belich quotes a private's diary discussing the dehumanizing effects of World War I: "It was being gunfodder material, mindless robots, that really got me." Although the word *robot* is derived from the Czech *robota* (meaning labor) and was used as a common term for a serf in Czech, outside of Karel Capek's play its first recorded use in English was in New York in 1923 (*Wikipedia*, s.v. "Robot," http://en.wikipedia.org/wiki/Robot). Belich offers no further details about the private in question, although there is the possibility that he may have been of Czech origins. Likewise, the entry might have been edited after 1923.

WORKS CITED

Alessio, Dominic. "Civilisation, Control and Co-operation: Picturing the Natives in the British Settlement Colonies (1870-1930)." *Journal of Imperial and Post-Colonial Historical Studies* 1, no. 1 (Spring 2000): 71-112.

———. "Close Encounters of the Earliest Kind: A Postcolonial Sighting of Aliens from the Planet Venus and the First Human Colony in Science Fiction (1881)." *ARIEL* 33, no. 1 (2002): 5-36.

———. "A Conservative Utopia? Anthony Trollope's *The Fixed Period* (1881)." *Journal of New Zealand Literature* 22 (May 2004):73-94.

———. "Gender, 'Race' and Proto-Nationalism in Julius Vogel's *Anno Domini 2000; or, Woman's Destiny* (1889)." *Foundation* 91 (Summer 2004): 36-54.

———. "*The Great Romance*, by The Inhabitant." *Kōtare* 2, no. 2 (November 1999): 3-17.

———. "*The Great Romance*, by The Inhabitant." *Science Fiction Studies* 20, no. 3 (November 1993): 305-40.

———. "*The Great Romance*: A Science-Fiction/Utopian Novelette, Part One." *Kōtare* 1, no. 1 (October 1998): 59-101.

———. "*The Great Romance*: A Science-Fiction/Utopian Novelette, Part Two." *Kōtare* 2, no. 1 (May 1999): 48-79.

Alkon, Paul K. *Science Fiction before 1900*. Oxford: Maxwell Macmillan International, 1994.

Amis, Kingsley. *New Maps of Hell: A Survey of Science Fiction.* London: Victor Gollancz, 1961.

Bagnall, A. G., ed. *National Bibliography of New Zealand to the Year 1960.* Vol. 1. Wellington: Shearer, 1969.

Baker, David. *The History of Manned Space Flight.* London: New Cavendish Books, 1981.

Belich, James. *Paradise Reforged: A History of the New Zealanders; From the 1880s to the Year 2000.* Honolulu: University of Hawai'i Press, 2001.

Bellamy, Edward. *Looking Backward, 2000–1887.* New York: New American Library, 1960. First published 1888 by Houghton Mifflin.

Blanchard, Jerrold, and Gustave Doré. *London: A Pilgrimage.* Hertfordshire, UK: Wordsworth Editions, 1987. First published 1872 by Grant & Co.

Bleiler, Everett F. *Science-Fiction: The Early Years.* Kent OH: Kent State University Press, 1990.

Bowman, Sylvia E. *Edward Bellamy Abroad.* New York: Twayne, 1962.

Clute, John, and Peter Nicholls. *The Encyclopedia of Science Fiction.* London: Orbit, 1999.

Davis, J. C. *Utopia and the Ideal Society: A Study of English Utopian Writing 1516–1700.* Sydney: Cambridge University Press, 1983.

Fairburn, Miles. *The Ideal Society and its Enemies: The Foundations of Modern New Zealand Society, 1850–1900.* Auckland: Auckland University Press, 1989.

———. "The Rural Myth and the New Urban Frontier." *New Zealand Journal of History* 20, no. 9 (1975): 3–21.

Gibbons, P. J. "The Climate of Opinion." In *The Oxford History of New Zealand*, edited by W. H. Oliver with B. R. Williams, 302–32. Oxford: Oxford University Press, 1984.

Goldberg, David Theo. *Racist Culture.* Oxford: Oxford University Press, 1993.

Hennessey, R. A. S. *Worlds Without End: The Historic Search for Extraterrestrial Life.* Gloucestershire, UK: Tempus, 1999.

Inhabitant, The. *The Great Romance.* Ashburton: *Ashburton Guardian*; Dunedin: *Otago Daily Times*, 1881.

Klarer, Mario. "Woman and Arcadia: The Impact of Ancient Utopian Thought on the Early Image of America." *Journal of American Studies* 27, no. 1 (1993): 1–17.

Lipow, Arthur. *Authoritarian Socialism in America: Edward Bellamy and the Nationalist Movement.* Los Angeles: University of California Press, 1982.

Introduction

MacKenzie, John M. *Orientalism: History, Theory and the Arts*. Manchester: Manchester University Press, 1995.

Macnie, John. *The Diothas*. New York: Arno, 1971. First published 1883 by G. P. Putnam's Sons.

Mann, Phillip. "Science Fiction." In Robinson and Wattie, *New Zealand Literature*, 482.

McGregor, Russell. *Imagined Destinies: Aboriginal Australians and the Doomed Race Theory, 1880–1939*. Melbourne: Melbourne University Press, 1997.

McLauchlan, Gordon. "An End to Cultural Thumb-Sucking." Review of *The Great New Zealand Argument: Ideas About Ourselves*, edited by Russell Brown. *New Zealand Books* 15, no. 4 (October 2005): 8.

McLeod, John. *Beginning Postcolonialism*. Manchester: Manchester University Press, 2000.

Miller, Paul. "Bell, Col. George William." In Robinson and Wattie, *New Zealand Literature*, 51.

Miller, Ron. "The Spaceship as Icon: Designs from Verne to the Early 1950s." In Ordway and Liebermann, *Blueprint for Space*, 49–68.

Morgan, Arthur E. *Edward Bellamy*. Perspectives in American History 18. Philadelphia: Porcupine, 1974.

Moskowitz, Sam. Introduction to *Across the Zodiac: The Story of a Wrecked Record*, by Percy Gregg, i–vi. Westport, CT: Hyperion, 1974.

———. "The Growth of Science Fiction From 1900 to the Early 1950s." In Ordway and Liebermann, *Blueprint for Space*, 69–82.

Ordway III, Frederick I. "Dreams of Space Travel From Antiquity to Verne." In Ordway and Liebermann, *Blueprint for Space*, 35–48.

———. "The Rocket From Earliest Times Through World War I." In Ordway and Liebermann, *Blueprint for Space*, 85–94.

Ordway III, Frederick I., and Randy Liebermann, eds. *Blueprint for Space: Science Fiction to Science Fact*. Washington DC: Smithsonian Institution, 1992.

Parrinder, Patrick. "Entering Dystopia, Entering Erewhon." *Critical Survey* 17, no. 1 (2005): 6–21.

Pierce, John J. *Foundations of Science Fiction*. London: Greenwood, 1987.

———. *Great Themes of Science Fiction*. London: Greenwood, 1987.

Pieterse, Jan Nederveen. *White on Black: Images of Africa and Blacks in Western Popular Culture*. London: Yale University Press, 1992.

Porter, Dennis. "Orientalism and its Problems." In *Colonial Discourse and Post-*

Colonial Theory: A Reader, edited by P. Williams and Laura Chrisman, 150–61. New York: Columbia University Press, 1994.

Pringle, David, ed. *The Ultimate Encyclopedia of Science Fiction: The Definitive Illustrated Guide*. London: Carlton Books, 1996.

Robinson, Roger. Introduction to *Anno Domini 2000; Or, Woman's Destiny*, by Julius Vogel, 11–21. Auckland: Exisle, 2000.

———. "Erewhon or Over the Range." In Robinson and Wattie, *The Oxford Companion to New Zealand*, 166–67.

Robinson, Roger and Nelson Wattie, eds. *The Oxford Companion to New Zealand Literature*. Oxford: Oxford University Press, 1998.

Roth, Herbert. "Bellamy Societies in Indonesia, South Africa, and New Zealand." In *Edward Bellamy Abroad*, edited by Sylvia E. Bowman, 226–57. New York: Twayne, 1962.

Said, Edward W. *Orientalism*. London: Penguin, 1991. First published 1978 by Vintage Books.

Salmond, Anne. *Two Worlds: First Meetings between Maori and Europeans 1642–1772*. London: Penguin, 1991.

Sargent, Lyman Tower. *New Zealand Utopian Literature: An Annotated Bibliography*. Wellington: Stout Research Centre, 1996.

Shelley, Mary. *Frankenstein*. Harmondsworth: Penguin, 1994. First published 1818 by Harding, Mavor & Jones.

Sobchak, Vivian. *Screening Space: The American Science Fiction Film*. 2nd ed. New York: Ungar, 1987.

Sorrenson, M. P. K. "Maori and Pakeha." In *The Oxford History of New Zealand*, edited by W. H. Oliver and B. R. Williams, 168–96. Oxford: Oxford University Press, 1988.

Stone-Blackburn, Susan. "Consciousness Evolution and Early Telepathic Tales." *Science Fiction Studies* 20, no. 2 (July 1993): 241–50.

Suvin, Darko. *Metamorphoses of Science Fiction: On the Poetics and History of a Literary Genre*. New Haven: Yale University Press, 1979.

Thomas, Nicholas. *Colonialism's Culture: Anthropology, Travel and Government*. Oxford: Polity, 1994.

Wedderspoon, Richard. *The Dominion of New Zealand, Britain's El Dorado of the Southern Hemisphere*. Christchurch, New Zealand: Simpson & Williams, 1927.

Winter, Frank H., "Planning For Spaceflight: 1880s to 1930s." In Ordway and Liebermann, *Blueprint for Space*, 104–12.

A Note on the Text

In the republication that follows, noticeable typesetting, grammatical, and spelling errors have been changed for the sake of clarity. Although the original spellings have been retained, the occasional distinct misspelling has been noted for the sake of interest. While the general preponderance of semicolons, commas, extended sentences, and dashes in the original has been preserved, in order to remain as true as possible to the original style, there are places where excessive and awkward overuse has been amended to improve the text's readability.

The Great Romance

Volume 1

———

I
WILL
TELL YOU
A TALE WILDER
THAN POET EVER DREAMED!
YEA, STRANGER THAN
THE VISION OF
THE MADDEST
PROPHET!

TO JOHN KEATS,
TO WHOSE MEMORY
THE VOLUMES OF THE GREAT ROMANCE ARE
RESPECTFULLY DEDICATED

O, thou whose voice, as from the setting sun,
As from the land where old gods deathless lie,
Poured in my heart like an Archangel's trump,
Wakening a deathless memory, which to day,
The offspring of past blisses and deep joys
Unto the outer air doth feebly cry.

O, hush in billowy volumes, low and sweet
As love and birth, passion and strange pain mixed
The sound doth creep, yea folds me round
As I have felt, when past the light of day,
The darkness dumbly creep into my brain,
A prelude dim and strange as of eternal sleep.

1

"What is it?" I said.

I awoke and tried to collect my thoughts. Before me stood a man; I don't like to confess it, but a glance told me a much better man than myself.

I was just awakened. Then gradually there stole into my mind the past facts.

"What year is it?" and the man lifted his eyes and looked straight into mine. Was he a mesmerist? Something from his look seemed to wander around my brain and try to find an entrance.

"Two thousand one hundred and forty-three," I said. A ridiculous guess, I thought at the same moment.

Again the man lifted his eyes, and before I could think again I said to myself, "You are right."

I was abashed, and turned my eyes to the ground. Then it all came back to me.

In the year 1950 my dearest friend, John Malcolm Weir, the greatest chemist of his day, had given me the sleeping draught: it should tie up the senses—life itself—for an indefinite period; and when the appointed years were over life might again be awakened.

Yes, I recollect, I was depicted in *Punch* as the "Sleeping Beauty," just a week or two before I went off. Yes, and John Weir on the next page, drinking the elixir of life, while, with his finger on his nose, his thumb pointed me out in the corner. Yes, *Punch* started three large-sized engravings just before. I suppose wit was growing more plentiful. Moxton had the third—great chemist, too, great everything—the philosopher's stone, but that was not so good. *Punch* could only write *Coal* on one heap and *Gold* on another. I always advocated his going into colours; but—what? Did someone speak? Did someone say . . .

"The one thing we have not yet found out?"

I looked at my companion. He had grand eyes, and now they were bent on me with a wonderful power and interest.

"Confound the man, does he think I am a woman?" My hand naturally sought my chin; the large growth of hair quite relieved me. I looked again. The man before me looked up. He had evidently been blushing. I looked hard. Good God! He had no hair on his face; he was very young. His eyes fell to the ground. His garments were the garments of a man; but—what—I must confess my thoughts did wander wild. Yet, as my eyes returned and once again met his—yes, his—I knew it instantly. If I had been sleeping a thousand years I should have known it. If I had been lying on a couch for ten thousand years I should have jumped up, as I did then, as he advanced towards me.

"Why will you make me speak? Why do you think so animal-like of woman? If you have no curb for your spirit, know that almost every one you meet can read your thoughts."

We are startled out of exclamation and fear when some sudden immense fact breaks like light on the mind. I looked hard at my companion as he stood before me. A wondrous, glorious feeling—awe, benevolence, love, enjoyment, seemed to come round about me, almost to enter into my life, as I met his steady gaze.

I was on the point of speaking; something—I cannot recollect what—was rising in my brain, when he again opened his lips.

"Why do you want to speak?"

I could only gaze in astonishment.

He continued, "I thought it must be so." Then, in a still sweeter tone, he said, "We do not often speak now," and, as his face grew troubled, "Your mind is more than irregular; try to cleanse and calm it while only I am here; it will hurt you else in after years to think that others saw it thus. Yes, I believe it would have been better to have made your sleep death, soon after your friend left this world; but the older men would not hear of it. You first started the mechanical world on this new track. You found out that power which so swiftly drives us through the air and over the earth; so, not to seem ungrateful even to a straying thought, we let you sleep on."

I have many times felt a thrill of pleasure when, in doubt or difficulty, a trusted friend has taken my hand, and I have been assured that through everything he would stand by me. But that was but a semblance—a faint sketch—of the thrill that went through me as my companion stretched out his hand to me, and a voice seemed to wind round me again, saying, "Think nothing you would be ashamed to put into words and acts; no, not even in a desert, for, though your friends may be now on the other side of the world, they may afterwards catch the imprint of your thoughts." But yet the man was only looking at me. It was confusing.

I said to him, "How old are you?"

He would not speak, but smiled.

I said to myself, "Twenty-one."

"Yes," he replied, "cannot you think with me?"

But as I did not answer, he went on, "We need not to speak for utility, only when we wish for the melody of the voice; we can read so well each other's thoughts, conversing for hours, without a word."

"Oh!" said I, "that was one of the things *Punch* never thought of, and if he had I don't know how he would have managed it."

"Ah, *Punch*," said my companion. "An old, old paper; we keep it going yet, but we have regulated his features considerably."

I was still looking at the young man, but as he mentioned the features of *Punch* an idea of my own looks stole before me. I was conscious of ugliness, but I recollect I was not thought an ill-looking man; never saw my bad points before.

These thoughts, though they take time to read, took no appreciable time to think.

My companion instantly began, "I beg your pardon, sir—forgive my rudeness."

"What do you mean?" said I.

He answered, "I ought, perhaps, to warn you, as I think this may be a new trouble. Sir, this time which you have slept has helped [bring] on fast the work on which you must have noticed [in] the beginning; re-cast the human face and figure, improved it—beautified it." And again the man smiled, with an earnest, beautiful expression. I doubt not many pleasant thoughts were passing in his mind, but I could catch none of them. Then he went on.

"You will suffer most from women; when they see you, often, often, I fear, will their thoughts revert to your looks (this young man was just twenty-one). Their minds are less controllable than man's. If you read our best photographic histories you will learn that when men began to read each other's thoughts, all thoughts that were not good or inharmonious had to be banished, at first only with friends, then everywhere. The man that passed you in the street would turn round to look at you. Then it was too late, he knew your thoughts. And now no place is safe for any evil; as your thoughts grow strong—and all evil things do, ere they bloom to fruition—they get rampant, like a weed in a garden; then some other mind catches the vibration, and the world knows crime is almost impossible, for great deeds of wickedness would appear written on the brain in shining letters. Men have asked to be destroyed for very shame, men with great minds, too, yet so mixed with vile relics of the past that they were in a perpetual hell."

I thought, half-bitterly, that I should like to go to them. I suppose the man read my thoughts, for he seemed to answer them.

"'Ah, yes', I said to my father, 'it were better.' As I looked on you I said, 'Ah, why should he ever wake?'"

A cold feeling ran over me as he said these words.

"But you would not kill a man for thinking evil?"

The start, the flush, the look of bewilderment did me good.

"Kill a man before he wished to die! Do I interpret your thoughts? Why should we not go back and eat the human flesh, and drink the blood? Oh, faugh. Do not think thus. Oh, banish that worst relic of the past, that ignoble ["disennobling" in the original] fear, which has scarce so appeared in the human face this half century"—he checked himself a little—"at least not among the higher races."

"But," I said, "where are those men now? What did you do with them?"

"Some are yet struggling around this world, some will even drink of the *aqua vitae*. Like you, they fear to lose their being. It is for them, however, sad and hard, and they gradually lose respect, for the new generations are moulded to the present time: beautiful, strong—and I must use for you the old word—holy. He who outlives nature's limits, except under peculiar circumstances, is thought to be fearful—a weak man. Yet I tell you this, amongst the younger men and women, the old idea of perpetual life is reviving, and although we have never flown beyond this planet, only perfected our thought, we are dreaming now of other worlds—of Mars and Venus. Could we reach them and inhabit them, life might again increase. I don't think we should feel degraded, at least for two or three hundred years."

Oh, what a wild hope sprang up in my heart as he spoke these words. And then he smiled as he continued:

"Some rash philosophers say that we are perfection, that it was the change from speech to thought that so swiftly altered the human type; the change from half evil to good, by that made necessary, which so improved the human features. But all these things we leave to time, or until another genius like you shall come."

"Sir," I said, "let me think a little." As he still looked at me, "Leave me. I am amazed by what I have heard."

He said to me, "Though I leave you I shall be near you. My mind is already strung to your pitch and resounds to your every thought. I shall know whither your thoughts tend."

I answered, "Though you may I shall be to myself alone. I do not yet feel influenced by your mind, except you, as it were, speak to me."

He closed the light from his face—the expression.

I felt intensely relieved. He gave me a draught and went out. I drank, and, for the first time since I arose from my long sleep, I seemed awake.

2

I was alone. Thought—the free motion of the brain—began pleasurably to stir within me. Weir—yes, if I could only see him now. If he could only see me.

I can recollect how the old man's hand trembled as he gave me the last draught. 'Twas my death to him. He knew that a few more years would finish his career, and we had been fast friends so long.

Then—Oh Heaven!—with what vigour the new thought rushed in—that centuries had passed, that the deed had been done. The old world was now in the background; all the old faces, friends, gone.

Yet I lived. Alive? Well? Yes, to see, to know more than I had ever dreamed of.

I had an intense desire to rush abroad, to see the men and women. Glorious, beautiful faces rolled away past me in the stream of imagination. To see—everything. What, I could scarcely conceive.

Yet I would not. I would think first—wait till I heard more.

My companion's talk had made me feel almost like a prisoner. I had pictured to myself ere I slept, that my awakening would be like the crowning of a king; the world would be wondering at it. Yet, now it had come, what was I?

One of those great epochs of time—I might say the second—had passed over the world. The first made man a knowledgeable animal, to know good and evil; the second made him to know not only his conscious self, but also all others around him, to read their thoughts like open books, and that, in sequence, had brought on the dream of past time—THE GOLDEN AGE.

Yes, even though there were still, amid it all, those who wished themselves blotted out of existence.

Surely by this time they should be able to visit the planets—the little group of worlds swimming, not so far away. What had my companion said? They talked of it; it was not done yet, but then he had not told me all.

When I recalled his manner I felt a conviction that this also was soon to be accomplished, and then! and there! would we find a nobler race or a wide empty world? Had the creative power chosen this earth alone for its battlefield with the dead inertness of matter? Left the rest of the solar system for our increase, for the increase of those godlike moving beings, where not only dust stood, a symbol of beauty and life, but where to an immense extent, power was transmuted into pleasure?

I saw that though I could not read the mind of my late companion I had been sensibly affected. A semi-knowledge, which was not thought, was wandering through my brain—a dim, beautiful idea of intense mental pleasure, a pleasure which made friends happier than lovers;—and, lovers, can you imagine a sea of glory, a stream of intense moving rapture, yet self-conscious with beautiful calmness and a delicate unfaltering perception? My spirit was wondering at its own imaginations.

'Twere good indeed that this people should reach out to the stars and fill the vacant world with emphatically the Glory of God!

While I was thus thinking a woman opened the door and stood before me.

I was (that is before I slept) about fifty-six years old. I had known women in every form and phase. In my other life I had lived twelve years with one whose features I yet recall bent with a halo of beauty and kindness; yet this woman swept completely all other thoughts or imaginations, joys or sorrows, from my heart; her look—like that one might bend on some noble yet wounded beast struggling bravely for its life amid pain and partial helplessness. Yet so much more; I felt huge pulses throbbing about my head, of whose existence I had not been before aware.

She came near to me. She stretched out her hand, and as I took it, I seemed to begin to know thousands of events, people's acts, some past, some present, but all indistinct, dim, yet thrilling my heart with exquisite pleasure.

Moved by instinct—for who could think with such a face, such eyes, before them?—impelled by instinct, I say, I moved from off the couch, I know not how, still holding that divine hand, and whether I tried to steal my arm around her, or [a] kiss as I pressed that hand, or whether either went beyond thought—or whether both were madly mixed and produced a strange position, I cannot tell; but what I know is, that that calm, yet intense face looked down on mine, without displeasure, and the words "Not yet," like the tones of a bell, fell from her lips.

I think the rush of thought and pleasure took away all power from me; I sank to the ground, and, with those glorious eyes still bent on mine, she sat beside me.

Then she began to speak in a wondrous voice, whose soft tones, though seemingly restrained to a level nigh monotony, roused my spirit like a song of freedom. During all that low-toned monologue, whose restful words flowed on in unchallenged certainty, my heart seemed to be moving beneath its old fetters—the past life—ready to rise and be one with the present, one in the great onward march to the great future.

"I often saw you sleeping, and read off the half-effaced thoughts of your past life. Long before you awoke your brain would respond to mine, and tell off, though in a broken manner, all your strongest desires—all your troubled longings; and now, as you begin to see, we know so much of each other, you may speak without fear of myself—of anybody—of others—as man would speak to man, or woman to woman, for we read the thought if we speak not the word, and you must come into this same state of liberty."

Then my heart called out so loudly that she must have anticipated the spoken words: "If I might but follow so fair a guide till I could stand in perfect equality on the great plain of this new life; if I could"—but, ah, my rising spirit fell back as the words—"NOT YET" again dropped alone in my heart, and her clear liquid eye looked so steadily into mine, that it fell back in wonderment.

"Listen," she said, and, in what seemed a secret corner of my heart, the old words "NOT YET" seemed again to rise, and the glimmering spark that flitted in her eyes told me she too heard it. That single word, "Listen!" seemed to be repeated in my spirit till it calmed it. Then the fair, clear voice began anew. "The passions, the varied emotions of our hearts have ever been used to build up the mind and empower the brain. We do not now dismiss or try to conceal our passions. Women are now educated that their feelings may live in their intensest strength, but always in fit place, environed with beautiful circumstances." "No," she said, as answering my thought, "not gold or pearls and grandeur, but beauty and pleasure of thought and coalescence of spirit, that could live alone in another world for years, and yet not [be] weary."

She rose to go, and my heart strove again to assert itself, and seemed to struggle to grasp some tangible object, to break that impenetrable calm, and extract—if but one word—from her unguarded heart. But, held by the spell of her being, it fell back, and, erecting a secret altar within itself, it there poured out its worship.

But not, as I thought, unknown. Even as she passed, a strange smile flitted on her features, and the words "NOT YET" seemed to ring anew over all my heart. A glorious mocking of my secrecy!

3

She was gone, yet her presence lingered. All the fair beauty of her pure thought, the ideal, the essence of her existence hung like a glamour over me, and, as after the other visit, I began to be aware of many things ere this unknown. While she was with me the full tide of her life seemed poured all about my heart, burying the landmarks of the past and swallowing up knowledge in emotion. But now, as I grew calmer, facts and incidents sprang up in my brain—knowledge that came as a dream, I knew not how. Were these things true? Or was my amazed soul beside itself? Were these indeed Alfred Malcolm Weir and Edith Weir—brother and sister, and the descendants of my best friend? And had they, while watching over me as sacred dust, read my thoughts? Yes, here at least I could recollect Edith Weir had said as much. Oh, Pride! Ambition! Glory! What are ye all when friendship and trust draw nigh and breathe upon the shipwrecked solitary spirit? Not more does the escaped mariner rejoice in the safety, the warmth, the comfort of the house of refuge, than did my naked soul. It seemed to escape from the perilous exposure and find in this relationship a cloak, a shelter, a refuge from its pitiless eye of the great world. Ah, yes—did I belong to another age? And was my spirit old, and gnarled, and full of crooked ways? Give me but a vision of that sweet face, and what else in my heart could be seen or known? What of any hatred or malice, or any uncharitableness, even by an eye Almighty? And rising up like little knobs left by the retreating waters, other thoughts appeared.

They, the people of the new world, knew this, and for this reason had that fair face looked so often on my sleeping features, had her strong soul so often tried to wind itself about the convolutions of my half-frozen brain. And, perchance, for this—but, ah! how dim and shadowy grew this imparted knowledge now!—for this she would be ever with me, and all her love be mine, to guide and comfort me, and make my coming life glad as that of those I should dwell among. And though it came from farther than an echo, "faint as the faintest breath on polished stone," it was indeed "a chance that would redeem all sorrows." Pay—ah, doubly pay for all the risk and dangers past. If it might be!

I was walking up and down in my apartment, still filled with my surging thoughts, when the man who first awakened me again came nigh.

I hear a knock at the door; I cry "Come in," and there we stood, with a new sense of relationship, face to face.

"Ah! I see," he said, "what you are thinking of. I am very glad that our relationship gives you some pleasure. 'Tis something like the trust and confidence we have in each other now. But you have not yet seen the outer world. Come."

I followed him outside. We seemed to be in the midst of an immense city. The streets were as thickly peopled as the old London streets, but they were four times their width and planted with trees along either side. And then the flying machines!—my eyes were ever straying aloft—they were sailing like swallows in the summer afternoon, beautifully shaped, glittering in the light. My companion turned to me. "Yes, they look well. I think we beat the birds now, in command, as well as in pace; but still the old principle holds good. *You* are in front of the time there."

Of course I accepted this with a graceful bow. But young Weir (for thus I began already to think of my new companion) continued:

"When I look at the sky oftentimes, and think that but for you, we might be yet grovelling on the earth, but for you, horses or men or cumbrous steam might be yet painfully turning up the hard earth and reaping the scant harvest, I wonder the world in general does not rise up and give you an ovation—show at least that they are not forgetful of those who thought and worked long ages ago. But here comes Moxton; let me introduce him."

Then I, John Brenton Hope, almost wished myself asleep again. I did. They looked at each other. I knew they were speaking; but that was not the thing that went into my heart. Up rose before me the woman's face I had seen, Edith Weir. I seemed to hear her name. I saw her—through Moxton's presence.

He looked out so hardly and proudly that minute, as though he would crush remorselessly every weak or unlovely thing, even though it were part of himself—Lucifer, but Lucifer triumphant, and as Byron imagined he would be in that case. I thought all this and much more in the second of time ere we were made known to each other. Of course the speaking was a condescension to my old-world weakness, which I thought they might almost have dispensed with; but was rather taken aback when Moxton said, as if answering me, "It were better."

I looked hard at him, as I had looked through many a man before.

He smiled and said, "I wonder in what manner we are alike?" Then, as I still gazed, "Edith Weir has taken so much of our thoughts."

I answered, "Charles Moxton, I do not quite comprehend all your meaning. I suppose you know all my thoughts. I only know some of yours, and even those seem to obey different laws, to be governed by different instincts to those common to the old world."

Alfred Weir interposed, "Moxton, you and I are the only men Hope has yet conversed with."

Then turning to me, "As soon as you become a little more accomplished in our language of thought you will read the laws of morals and manners in the mind of every one you converse with—not that they are difficult, the negative part is the lack of all you are ashamed of; the positive, as it is used, runs farther with some than with others."

"But what is this?" I said, as a huge building caught my eye, supported on pillars like a temple, but that the spaces between the pillars were filled by huge doors, some of which were open, and some shut. I should not have noticed it, perhaps, but for its being surrounded by a large open space about a quarter of a mile in width.

"Oh, the new shed for goods traffic," said Weir; "let us walk down and see the *Aphis* start." We passed several of the aërial boats standing on an inner railway, which circled several times round the enclosure.

In shape and fashion these boats were like the old blockade runners, their upper lines being as graceful as those of the hull; in fact, more so, for beneath, their symmetry was marred by the wheels on which they ran.

"Yes," said Weir, "if some fellow could get rid of gravitation we could improve their appearance." Then, as if struck with a sudden thought, he said, "I say, Charlie, pitch out that stick of yours."

"All right," said Moxton, with a smile; and he then threw it out twenty yards or so in front of us.

We stopped. The stick rose up and began to come steadily towards us—it had a curiously carved head and looked like a species of snake advancing.

Weir began to laugh, then going slowly toward it, motioned with his hands to push it back. It was absurd to see the head thrown back by every pass he made; yet, despite his efforts, it still made way, Moxton standing with just a touch of Lucifer on his countenance.

"Oh, come on," said Weir, as he came back to us, and the stick resumed its original motion; but suddenly it was dashed to the ground as by a gunshot. We both of us felt a slight shock.

I simply looked round, but Weir exclaimed, "I say, Moxton, you are getting as strong as a battery."

Moxton did not answer him, but seemed to be concentrating his energies. He said, "Now look."

The stick rose with its point in the air, then, dashing that to the ground, it came with a bound like a tumbler right into his hand.

"Oh Lord, Moxton," said Weir, as he took the stick and began facetiously to examine its head, "its eyes are growing, it will begin to eat next week; look," he said, handing it to me.

"Is it a trick?" I asked.

"No," answered Moxton, "magnetic power of no practical use at present. Try it, Weir. That stick," he said, as he handed it to Weir, "it is like an old violin, constant use has made it more easy to be penetrated by the magnetic power."

"But," I said, "we both felt the shock when you dashed it down."

"Yes," he replied with a smile, "all that you feel was dissipated, lost. But don't be a fool, Weir."

For Alfred Weir, after several vain attempts, had induced the inanimate bit of timber to follow him, retreating with his face still towards it, and giving it, as far as he was able, the motions of a frolicsome drunkard. Hearing Moxton's words, he brought it to grief on a rail in front of us, letting it lie, but I noticed it rose up by instinct into Moxton's hand as we walked over it.

"Here comes the *Aphis*," said Weir, as one of the huge doors rolled up and a beautiful, almost steel-blue vessel came slowly out.

"She is one of the largest yet built," said Moxton, as four immense pinions pushed themselves out from each side of the vessel. They shook the air for an instant with a tremulous motion, then poised themselves as the *Aphis* slowly glided ["guided" in the original] off on an outside track, which I could now see running round the enclosure. The wings remained poised, but the vessel's speed increased continually, so that ere she had travelled a mile she must have been going at the rate of a hundred miles per hour. As she again neared us, I saw her wings moving again faster and faster till the points faded from sight, and the whole pinion resolved itself into a flutter of air close to her body. Then she lifted herself steadily upwards, propelled forward as yet by her attained motion.

"Now she has her full swing," said Moxton, as the vibratory motion at her sides seemed suddenly to lengthen, and, even at our distance, we could see her dash forward with an immense accession of speed.

"You could almost visit a planet in a boat like that," said Moxton. "Yes," answered Weir, "that is what I proposed, but Moxton is afraid we should use him up as motive power if anything broke down or wore out. The only reason, I assure you, that kept us from starting."

Moxton observed, in a "to-those-whom-it-may-concern-manner," that Weir always made bad jokes when hungry.

So their minds are not always strung up to that intense height of thought. A decided feeling of relief, of relaxation, had been stealing over me during the walk; the childlike fun of my friends seemed to give me more assurance than I could have gathered even from a perfect knowledge of their thoughts. The only thing that disconcerted me was Moxton saying, with his eyes "Yes, men play now, and children think."

I had enough wit left, however, to say in the same manner, "Then, to which class do you belong?"

"We are as yet betwixt either."

And I knew there were further thoughts in his mind, which, perhaps, he did not intend me to catch, of how I was standing betwixt the old and the new, and, though living in the new world, only half its child. Half pained, my eyes strayed to Alfred Weir; there, too, the same strain of thought was playing. The face that looked on mine as when I first wakened.

Moxton broke up the reverie, "Suppose we go for your sister, Weir, and you dine with me?"

We agreed; and, hailing a carriage, we rolled swiftly away to the outskirts of the city.

What a brightness seemed to infuse itself around us with her presence. Each heavy thought, each hard, out-stretching idea, was put far away, a sweet pure stream of bright ideas, interspersed with words, musical and beautiful. And, though she gave by far the larger part of her attention to Moxton, there was what may be best described as a steady current of serenity flowing continually from her head to mine, and again I was aware that *my* appreciation of it heightened *her* enjoyment.

But if Edith Weir shed light around her, Lucy Moxton seemed to bring us into the region of sunshine, like the angels of life and death. When her brother introduced her to me, he, dark and tall, with every motion indicating power, her beautiful hair and sunlit face—yet, no, not life and death, but love and death—for Edith Weir was yet the embodiment of life to me, my guiding star.

I sat beside Lucy Moxton during that long and happy dinner hour, drinking in her flowing, bubbling thoughts, and rejoicing in her happy laughter.

"The old world was not so bad if all the men were like you."

I could not but rejoin, "The new world was indeed a paradise if all the women were"—but I did not even in thought conclude the sentence, and she knew the "you" was inclusive.

I described to her John Malcolm Weir and Wilsdon Moxton, whom I had known, ah, far better than I knew her brother and Alfred Weir.

The summer evening air stole in through the long open window. The level sunshine seemed to be caught and broken in the rustling leaves; to be born in to us among the faint sounds they awakened, and to mingle with the fine pleasure that, like an atmosphere, enveloped us.

As I look back on this time through the halo of time and the immense distances of space, on the old, new world, thronging with its almost glorious inhabitants, I wonder and try to forecast the future, my thoughts circling out in wider ranges, till the life of the universe and the mastery of creative power seemed only akin to the distant circling system, and almost within our grasp.

That was a strange evening. I remember walking out into the fairy-like garden with Lucy Moxton, while she told me some of the many incidents that passed in my sleep—how many had at first gazed at me; how unwise imitators had fallen through to the unawaking sleep; how it had been made criminal to give the draught of sleep; the names of great men; the coalescence of nations, the final triumph of sense over brute force; till in a soft, low voice, how Edith Weir with herself had watched the living relic of the past, and tried to read the last thoughts imprinted on the brain, of which, by the way, she startled me by saying, "We formed a chart, which I will show you some day." She repeated what I knew so well, of the affinity which they had discovered between the mind of Edith and my own, and then I remember walking in the holy twilight, the dim, beautiful glow, till the face of my companion seemed to be fading in the long distance, the darkness to creep into my brain. I seemed to feel it numbly as a noiseless prelude to death, and only saw among it, like a star, the face of Edith; then it closed over me.

5

But with the breaking day again came the full tide of sensation. 'Twas not so much the body as the brain, the press of ideas, the tide of thought, and then, perhaps, it was but that the meats and wines were not such as we used two hundred years ago.

Yet even as I became conscious, almost at once I heard a chorus of voices, and down the street came chanting ["chaunting" in the original] a troop of girls. In the clear morning air, in the delicious breeze—had I slept, and dreamed of yesterday? Had I awakened a thousand years back in this world's history? Such beautiful youth seemed not to belong to dreams of philosophy and the latter days. Yet they did. And many a morning since have I hovered in my aërial boat over the great city, and seen the troops of men and maidens, who would sing as they passed to their labours, strong and joyous with an intense vigour, that only required restraint. For, as I quickly saw, a few year's work in the early years of life sufficed to keep the world full and plenteous of all store, and many wrought on, some for pleasure, some ambition, and some for gain. And, though millions thronged the vast pleasure-grounds of Europe, and cities grew out like countries, there was enough, plenty, and as provision for inclement seasons, such immense stores that never were dreamt of in other days; but this is all what I saw and gathered later, and when rolling over the fertile plains of Africa, or watching the Amazon with its myriad streams.

I was for an hour with Edith that morning. She told me much concerning the social welfare of that day. She said, "You do not seem quite to understand that law and ceremony and promise are hardly needed now. Should a man deceive a woman not one in all these throngs you see would speak to him, whilst she would receive daily comfort; then each one marries young."

It was strange to see the frank smile which made the blush pleasurable as the young girl told me of all these things.

"But do you take one another for better or worse, richer or poorer?" She knew the rest, and said with a smile that seemed to becalm my brain, "Sometimes. The struggle for existence is really ended, and so much sweetness fills every relation of life, that the old sins and sorrows are gone; except"—she stopped. The first cloud I had seen swept over her brow—"there are some like the monks and nuns of old. They are not closed in by walls or pointed out by garments. They wander among the crowd; but they are bound by the voice of the world. They have no interest in the future, nor could they hardly wish to perpetuate their own existence."

Then I said to her, "This opening of the gates of thought has not swept away all weakness or unworthiness."

She looked one of those strange looks. "Do you understand impossibility? Can thought give you six fingers, or take away an inherited disease or deformity?" But she continued, "They have pleasure to the full, and though they have sympathy from the rest of the world, they oftener draw together. Their joy is wilder, but it seems to us like that of a drunkard."

It was with us, then, like Dante's lovers, when they ceased to read of the loves of Launcelot and the Queen. "Our eyes oftentimes grew together." Could it be possible that we should simply clasp hands and she would be mine—but she went away with a laugh, seeming to fling back on me a shower of thoughts—of stolen waters—and old world gallantries.

Then she came back and looked at me till a thin, freezing fear crept like despair around my heart. As I looked on her glorious form and triumphant features, the thought of my own meagre body and my face like that of one of those who are not fit for the battle of life, filled all my mind; but she came and gave me her hand as she had done when first I awakened, and then I doubly knew and felt and believed all her goodness, and in her thoughts I read that had the social decree doomed me to remain with the things of the past, doomed me never to mingle my own life with present and future, then other than her brother would have met me wakening, other than herself would have gazed on me sleeping. Yes, I was content.

"But did no one break these unwritten laws?"

"But rarely, and then they are put out of the commonwealth and live amongst those nations not yet incorporated in the kingdom of thought, the Hottentot, the degraded Negro, and the great border land of peoples."

"And are there many of these?"

"Yes, in numbers, but in proportion we are ten to one, and soon shall be a hundred."

As I talked with her, she seemed not so much the glorious creature of the new world, but a maiden with a strong, true mind, in whose love one could be—oh, how wonderfully—at rest, for before the morning was far gone, her brother and Moxton came for me.

The fertile brain—the power to do—next only to the power to be; that which guided the world a thousand years ago would guide it now. Were Shakespeare or Darwin now alive, still striding before the mass of humanity, their great minds would cast into farther recesses the rays of human knowledge. So I thought on the eventful morning—not yet a year above ground, for I seemed truly to be alive again, and was I—I—once again to launch the world into another cycle of progress? Or was it madness? Should we go wandering on in the pathless places of eternity? Should we meet the God of the Universe as we went out between the planets? Wonderful—more wonderful than were the present men and women to me and my eventful awakening. Then a host of details intruded—the expansive force of an atmosphere when in space; the greatest time we would supply ourselves with oxygen—down to the number of revolutions our winged wheels would make in space; and whether it would be safe to use the Yankee Eternal Lubricator. Or yet again—would she follow me to this new world, or had I had my day, the greatest reward this world could offer, and now its vastest tomb?

I thought of the happy hours, those dumb, unspeakably doubly sweet moments that had swept over us, when we drained to its dregs the cup of pleasure, and her hand seemed ever to fill it again. I longed for the old ties, even the prejudice, that would have bound her to me for good or ill. Yes, I longed passionately to return again to the old delicious bondage.

Yes, we all know it, this old longing for childhood's day again. Anything to be at rest, when tired with the upward struggle, and the upward struggle—with me—had been long. Yet could I be so selfish as to wish even for a moment that she should share the danger, the hardships of the first planetary voyage?

But why delay the coming moment? Three of us, Charles Moxton, Weir, and myself, were soon to start on that most eventful voyage.

John Weir, the father of the man I saw when awakened, came in to see me in the evening.

"Well, Hope, you are a fool," he said. "When there are hundreds of useless, dull-brained animals whose loss would be no detriment to anything, you must go and immolate yourself before the golden idol of fame."

I reminded John Weir that I had once before done the same thing and had arisen like a phoenix.

"Yes," he replied complacently, "death is fire, a whirlpool which sucks in all, but gives it not back. There is an old legend of Schiller's ["Schyler's" in the original], of the youth who plunged into the whirlpool for the golden cup of the king. He came back again with the cup, but when he attempted the feat a second time—"

"I know," I said, "but I thought it was your opinion that nature should take her course, and that we old world inhabitants should make room for the younger race."

"Yes," he said, "that is it, that is what you are struggling for. You are afraid to let nature take its course, you are strengthening your body with the perpetual elixir, forgetting the terrible struggle that may come on between life and death, forgetting even your disadvantages of form and face when compared with the present race, hoping to give yourself a right to perpetual life, hoping I know not what, some wild dream of founding another world in the distant planets, taking your own genius and two or three of the first men amongst us to certain destruction."

I looked at John Weir, and innumerable thoughts came crowding over me—weird, vague, intense, yet so thick, so fantastic, that I myself could not assimilate them.

"Yes," I repeated in my own mind, "even your form and face proclaim your disadvantage with the present race." I knew well he was thinking of his son and daughter, but not more vividly were their faces engraved on his memory than on my mind.

We sat and thought against each other. I of those men and women whose younger life I loved so well, whose aspirations seemed to touch a perpetual fountain in my breast, of the vast outlook of the future, the intense joys of which the human heart is capable. But during all the time I was aware of the strong counter-current of idea. The strong noble mind which willingly, firmly, resigned its entirety, satisfied to cease to be. The gravity in all its beauty which lingered so long in the features of the sphinx, and seemed to live anew in Grecian art, settled down on John Weir's countenance, as the full force of the idea swept from him to me. Then the thought rose up and seemed to cry aloud within me, as in revolt from the known sentence of his law. "It was but an hour ago and your greatest wish was peace and perfect rest."

What a grim, powerful smile illumining the old man's features as in his eyes this but weak thought like a crying child arose.

"Yes, you allow yourself to be flattered by your own mind, the wish for certain life and pleasure is put in the balance against the strength to resign all and yet be calm, and not self-complacent."

I felt beaten back like one who would leave a desolate island, yet wave after wave leaves him exhausted on the beach. Yet even in the moment, something—that unknown power which rises up with a resistless energy and assures us of victory—awoke and began to move. I felt the light break on my face and fall into the old man's eyes, before ever articulate thoughts were formed.

"To leave this greatest act to dull-brained fools, and my own thoughts to be wrought out by a stranger; to wait at home and count death; to send out on the wildest and furthest voyage ever dreamt of by man, those men of the present whose later birth had brought them nearer to the eternal harmonies. Yes, John Weir, though heaven and earth be now against me, I will see through my latest and brightest thought. I know the future will be for me, and if in yon world afar I can attain that endless being, which the present race seem to think me unfitted for, who, even in thought, can there render me aught but homage."

"Yes yes, so far 'tis well. 'Tis a noble thing for the caterpillar to live all through the summer, but can he refrain from envying the butterfly?"

And as he left, the looks of the girl and her father were mingled together in my spirit. I thought of the hour when first watched by those eyes that looked too deeply into mine. I saw, as in a dream through the countless ages, the eternal warfare of matter with spirit, the intensity of impossibility, and again I wished I had never awakened.

7

We had sped around the world, across oceans and continents, we had wandered away into space till the world looked dim and luminous. We had performed the greatest feat of the age, we had voyaged round the Earth's only satellite—ours was not the first, nor had ours like the others been only fraught with barren honour as we sailed slowly round that miniature globe, whose frost and sunshine and lifeless air we could not for a moment breathe, or live in.

All our thoughts were turned to the future, to our great attempt—not an empty feat, but the opening of a new world—bringing another planet beneath the sway of human intellect, perhaps to find another form of god-gifted life. Beings who were not human, yet—yet—yes, what could they be in form and feature? I—Moxton and Weir—for five months we should be rushing through space—a second ark. Would it carry life to another world? Should we reach Venus I had intended to stay while Moxton and Weir returned. Not that I wished—as old John Weir had hinted—to bring a second time the golden cup of life from the whirlpool of the unknown. We had each and all volunteered, and I was chosen. My two comrades would return. Then Weir would lead the second voyage, and were it practicable Edith and Lucy Moxton would come with others. The boats for the second voyage now were far advanced, ere the first one left the earth.

Our greatest danger lay in the meteors. The principal streams that circulated round the world were pretty well known, but should all that immense space be strewn with them, 'twould add another danger. We had established an intense magnetic current in the *Star Climber*—for that was her name—so that any metallic aëreolite would so affect our boat and be, unless very large, so affected itself, that a collision was at all events placed farther off. Thus, if you raised the *Star Climber* steadily on her third pair of pinions, or hovers, as they were named—say with her head to the north—she would spring backward at the rate of fifty miles an hour. Stop her and turn her round she would be at the North Pole in twelve hours. This, however, was nothing to our intense motive power. Fancy a humming bird five hundred feet long of burnished silvered steel. You may then begin to comprehend what the *Star Climber* was like. She was truly a glorious boat. Her main pinions ninety feet long, whose slowest motion was after the first five seconds invisible, whose fine steel feathered points and edges, though more delicate than the most fragile fan, could not even be bent by the human hand. Yet such was their flexibility and temper, that the last ten feet, the real pinion, was packed in a box scarce double the old fashion pillbox.

We never expected to use a hundredth part of our power. Once into space our acquired motion would not need augmenting till we came within the attraction of some other planet. Yet here lay our danger: we might perish miserably on some large but airless planet as the mad voyagers De Reef and Frenzy did on the moon. In vain their wings fanned the resistless air. They could spring from the ground, their momentum carried them a few hundred yards upwards, then slowly the gravitation of the little orb drew them back. The thin air was poisoned for them. With a third part admixed they could scarcely breathe; with all their powers exerted they just hovered; the meagre atmosphere did not extend three hundred yards, in that they could move, although but slowly, after once losing their acquired momentum. But of that they could not rise.

The wreck lies yet in one of the deep craters in the North Eastern Hollow. There, with their patent air suppliers, they walked out, trying to find material to re-supply their oxygen; and had they been as clever as they were daring I believe they could have existed for months; but with little practical knowledge, they soon saw their helplessness, and ceased to strive. Moxton was with the party who found and buried them, and he took us down to see the place.

"A grave in the moon," with a huge natural tombstone of black rock above it, and deeply engraved their names and cause of death.

Moxton said he thought for our benefit, as he never saw anyone wandering about there, and although we were sure of an atmosphere in Venus, there might be many unknown causes to drive us out from the new world.

Our offensive powers were certainly enormous. A cannon or mortar was almost built into the vessel, yet swivel-working with patent discharge, so that with its mouth in space it could pour forth such an incessant stream of fierce projectiles as might frighten the boldest adversary. It was also intended to use against any small mass we might meet with in space, and last, but not least, as a motive power if we needed it. Its range was between fifty and a hundred miles, and the explosive strength of the projectile only limited by its proximity of the enemy to ourselves.

Moxton used to say he could dissipate the moon if it was worth while, but as that would have necessitated an aërial snagging contract, or made still more unsafe the interstellar way, we persuaded him to turn his thoughts to other fields and let our little satellite still go on its way rejoicing.

We were very happy that last week, I and Edith. Her brother had wild spirits—his caricatures of our party, in which I and Moxton figured conspicuously, were, as he used to say, "If not heart rending, spirit shaking."

The *Star Climber* wildly diving through blue ice for some unattainable South Pole, while Moxton and I with feet firmly planted were holding her by the rudder.

Moxton succumbed to Venusian wiles, a fish-like maiden combing his hair—a man-fish, grim, in the distance.

Seven years after, John B. Hope, very seedy, twenty-four young half-fish, assorted sizes, two flabby creatures in the rear, he sings dolefully "Home, Sweet Home."

As the planets roll in space, as the world turns its varied features to day and to night, with insensible motion, and as the solar system is swiftly moving in its predestined ["predistinated" in the original] course, noiselessly, silently, without even a rush of air around, so when our little bark shot into space, the noise, the throng, the sea of faces were gone. The fleet of air boats which hovered about us so long fell off one by one. We were alone.

Then the throb of our machinery was silenced. We had left the attraction of the world, had become as it were, an independent atom of the universe, had joined the grand march in the old world heavens, could see our natal world, now an orb, hung in the air.

We all knew the sensation—this loss of gravitation—this general unstability—this strange silentness, had felt it before. Yet it now seemed to quadruple its force. Perhaps it was the thought of danger, the knowledge, the realisation of how much—well nigh certain life and happiness—we were leaving behind, were risking for the air-bubble of fame, futurity. Yet this did not last long. We wished afterwards it had held us longer. Our brains were tired with the inevitable inactivity. We were forced to take refuge in work before the first incident broke the monotony of our journey.

One of us was always in our watch tower, with an intense electric light ready to turn in any direction, piercing for miles and miles the wonderful half-lit purple gloom that enveloped us—the gloom that was not darkness, yet want of light. We could see both the sun and stars shining, yet it was not light. The want of something to catch and stay those arrowy beams made the realms of space seem dim to us.

This was the thirtieth day of our journey. So far everything had prospered—all our machinery worked beautifully. An even temperature, which did not vary, except at our pleasure; our supply of air equal to that of a new country, and our speed, as we found from observations, had not slacked since the second day we left the earth, or since we had been entirely free from its attraction. We had met no meteor, no aëreolite had dashed across our way, both our offensive and defensive instruments were as when we parted from our last friends, and all our munitions of war were as yet in full stock. But this day, as I looked out of our watch tower, I saw right ahead of us, an increase in the darkness—an aërial fog bank—a Magellan cloud; and as we got nearer, it stretched away farther than the eye could see on every side. We then threw forward the intensest light of our electric lamp. Its rays seemed to touch it and stop, yet we knew from a variety of tests, it (the Magellan cloud) had no substance, not the least attractive power, and though earlier we could have avoided this huge—devil, Moxton called it. And, as we afterwards found it—canker in the universe; this death of matter, as death here is the death of life; this unutterable thing, which dissolved all things, everything—not into their original atoms, but into itself, into vacuity, nothingness. We could have avoided it—but before we had made up our minds, the intense speed of our noble boat carried us into its midst. No ray of light pierced it—a sense of unnerving fear swept over us and vibrated from soul to soul as we found ourselves in this unknown thing.

Moxton was the first to recover himself. He quickly took our instrument provided for the purpose of testing the exterior air, which could be thrust out as you push out a telescope, then opened, enclosed a small sample of the atmosphere and could be withdrawn. This Moxton did and detaching it, placed it in a glass vacuum chamber, and opened it. But what was our surprise and horror to see a small black patch float out into the receiver. It was then Moxton gave it the name. "It's a bit of that old-fashioned thing," he said, "the devil." But his eyes were not, as ours, on the curious little black cloud, but on the outside of the instrument in which he had caught it. His strong thought dragged our eyes there too. Although it had been exposed but a few seconds to this infernal gloom, it was cankered, its polished surface dulled and roughened. We drew down part of our signal staff, which was also of polished steel. Into it also this infernal atmosphere was marauding, and we comprehended in an instant our awful danger, for the whole exterior of our beautiful boat must be in the same manner disintegrating. This unreal blackness must be feeding among all her delicate wings, weakening each minute her glorious frame. Quicker than any word could be spoken we all knew our best course—our only hope. Moxton opened the box in which lay the springs of our defensive powers. "Hold on," he said, then laid his hands on the springs of our defensive organs. Though prepared for the effect, the rebound that in this thin air would drive us so fiercely onward, and gripping [what] was within our reach, both Weir and I were thrown well nigh the length of the cabin. The constant and enduring recoil of the perpetual discharge trebly accelerated the *Star Climber*'s speed, and although she weighed, say a hundred tons, there was absolutely nothing to stop her. For ten minutes did the smoking stream of fire and noise bellow through, and fight in this horrible space—then Moxton again touched the handles, and the voice of our deliverer ceased. The speed we had attained must be frightful yet the hideous darkness was yet around us. The minutes seemed hours, for we knew we were going faster than a shot from a gun, then at the same second the same thought penetrated us. I sprang to our lookout tower, closing down the outer casement, made haste to disconnect one of the glasses, while Moxton turned to our stores for a new one. But Weir, though later in thought, was quicker in action. With a turn of a handle, which was close to us, he sent the electric current through our outside signal lamp, and as the light came back, blurred and faint through our roughened half-decayed windows, we knew we were out of that horrible gloom, for as we entered it Weir had tried this same lamp, but then not one of those glorious vibrations had come back, all had been quenched by that enemy of nature and life.

We adjusted the new glass, threw back the outer casement, and there, behind us, lay the horror we had passed through—a black fog bank stretching away on either side farther than the eye could reach, and in height and depth it filled from Zenith to Nadir the purple Heavens.

This starlit gloom, this mock sunshine seemed now like a home. We rejoiced and felt safe in it; but, before anything else, we must make exact observations and know our rate of speed; also how much we should need to alter our course, for we were not rushing on to a fixed spot, to an oasis in the desert of the heavens, but to a wandering star that was here and there, or still farther on, according to the hour at which you sought it. We could not rush madly on, or we should reach the place appointed weeks before the planet spun its immense mass thither. It was a long and anxious time ere we could say with certainty we were again right, and fix the precise hour and spot of our meeting ground.

At last it was done. We knew our position, had replenished our instruments, and ascertained as far as possible the damage done to the exterior [of] our gallant craft. We had spread out her silvery wings, and though their beauty was gone, they were practically uninjured. In the air of the planet we had left I think we could even now go near to five thousand miles per hour, although their delicate edges were frayed and ragged, just as if we had been in a bath of some strong acid for ten minutes.

As for our appearance, it must surely be something like Coleridge's idea of the "Ancient Mariner's" bark. If our sails were not, our wings certainly were "thin and sere;" and should we again re-visit the glimpses of our natal moon we might startle more than "the pilot and the pilot's boy."

We were all thinking of our past danger, Moxton keeping his watch, gazing into the infinite space before him. He suddenly began to give us the moral of our last danger and escape. "There seems to be no limit to the speed we might attain in space, and if so, then distance becomes annihilated, and the whole universe open to us. There are other suns, and doubtless around them systems of planets such as we find here, but"—here he turned sharply round, "let us examine our friend the devil." Intimating in this coarse manner his wish to try some experiments on our little black genii—the handful of cloud we had fortunately secured.

We spent some little time in finding its specific gravity, or in trying to—but as we might have guessed, like the element it floated in, it was lighter than the lightest gas. We introduced a little common air, and soon observed a faint brown envelope all over the black mass, and by the aid of our instruments a slight sound between crackling and frizzling, evidently some chemical action going on.

After confining our friend in a still smaller compass we took from our small stock of living creatures a mouse and introduced it; we might as well have put it into a bath of prussic acid—its death was instantaneous. The effect on it being much the same as though it had been put through a flame.

To think of a world, like the one we had left, plunging into such a mass as it came rushing through space. A garden of Eden—a desolate wilderness would be nothing to the brightness and beauty and life before, the canker eaten blackness, the universal death behind. There would be no time for thought; like a black fogbank it would loom—then sweep over all with awful swiftness—and amid unutterable darkness the stinging vapour would lap everything to its destruction—and presently the world would ride forth to the outer day with its load of lifelessness—and creative work must begin anew.

"But," said Moxton, "perhaps the envelope of air would protect the planet, and all this destruction be reduced to a frizzling match some miles above us—in which the ancient deities ought to be more interested than the mundane inhabitant. All this, however, our little friend would probably enable us to find out—like the witches of old and all other scions of wickedness, when caught. A lively time would be in store."

And we, like an earlier-aged pilgrim, went on our way rejoicing—having, we believed, escaped from our Giant Despair, nearing we hoped, a better country.

Weir said, "Suppose we find the angels there."

Moxton, "Suppose it is inhabited."

I answered, "In that case most of our hopes will be disappointed. We must seek another planet—for earth's over-crowded happiness—perhaps before our search is ended it will lead us even to another system."

"Yes," answered Weir, "if we return from this first journey."

For the great globe of Venus was daily growing huger before us, like a moon at three-quarter's full it now appeared—yet not so clear as the earth's attendant; with our strongest glasses we could see both mountain, plain, and water; clouds, too, sometimes could be distinguished, altering the appearance of whole tracts of country and making us doubt our geography.

Our spirits grew buoyant, and a strange hope uplifted us day by day, that our enterprise would be successful. I think we began now to realise "the wonder of our work." Day had followed day with such unenviable calmness, as we walked up and down our gangway, but there was always an undercurrent whispering "Is it a reality, or but a dream, are you in the *Star Climber* amidst boundless space, or are those centuries of sleep unfinished, and are the dreams in that long night so real, John Bredford [sic] Hope."

Moxton and Weir knew all this—far more satisfactorily than I could gather their thoughts.

Moxton said to me, "You do not lose much—we are fuller of ideas than thought; our minds are like new wine strong and fiery, they want the glamour of age—the charm of long experience."

So we sped on, piercing the boundless, trackless space, that long purple gloom, where day follows day, and night, night, all wrapped in the same cold sunshine. Since the eternal ages dawned and the vast matter of this universe was gathered into orbs, those same swift vibrations had rushed through the thin air carrying heat and life to the bounds of the system.

And were it possible that other vibrations could travel swifter even than the beams of the sun, unseen yet no less real, I might have said that from the old world streamed a sweet influence. How well I remember it, as if some archangel had poured out a vial of sweet peace over my troubled heart. The influence wrapped and crept like the thickening mist of evening around my spirit, and that night, as Moxton and Weir slept, was, and is, one of the sweetest I ever lived.

Edith seemed to be always near me in her every beauty, sweeping all thought and care from the troubled brain, and when that influence faded like the red in the sunset, an intense peace seemed left. Such a mind as one would wish the spirit to possess when it quits this body of life, that whether, like a seed cast off from the tree of Humanity to find a rooting place in some other matter; or to be wafted, perhaps, on the ocean of infinity through long ages, till it drift ashore in some other world, and began again to mould the material by that, which, to our sense, is not, or like a spark it flitted out in darkness.

The old past days [of] my earliest life all revived and ran through my brain; but not in wild disorder, the influence in which they moved never waned, not even the monotonous morning could affect it, though, instead of clouds and dew and rising light and shadow and mists and an awakening world, the same dreary night light poured its unvarying sunshine over us, the monotonous air all about us, and around the nicely finished interior of the *Star Climber*.

Weir kicked it the other day, wished for a toothache, said that pain would come to be considered an epicureism, a dainty, a mental olive. Then sat down and calculated that for more than two full days we should have to career around our destined landing place. Skimming the thin air—most likely diving in and out of the atmosphere—getting rid as fast as we could of our superabundant speed. This was largely owing to our friend of whom we bottled a portion.

"But even then," Moxton said, "we should be large gainers. Our increased pace having saved us some hundreds of hours, and as yet given no larger risk."

In truth we had not sighted or felt a meteor—the chances of meeting one seemed less than that of a collision between the water going ships on the ocean.

10

We were old travellers. We knew the heavenly way; we had e'er this left the attraction of our native orb; we had seen with wondering eyes another world growing out and becoming immense before us, till it suddenly filled the whole horizon. We had heard the sharp sounds of the first thin air as we rushed through it, but that experience did not quiet our beating hearts, as we eagerly watched for the critical moment, when we must check that headlong plunge which our vessel would appear to make as the huge force of gravity again enfolded us.

We were fully conscious of, yet not able to realise the intense speed of our vessel. The pace at which we left the earth might be roughly estimated at twenty miles per second, not that we moved at that enormous speed in the earth, but we entered space, not only with our proper motion, but with that of the world we left added—viz., that mighty speed which annually brings winter and summer, and carries the earth and all its inhabitants some six hundred millions of miles in the year, and its smaller, yet not despicable diurnal motion, which might be roughly estimated at a thousand miles per hour. Of both these motions we were enabled by the course we chose to take the largest possible advantage. Thus we were not laggards, even by comparison, with the giant orbs we were among. Then our adventure in the Magellan Cloud had superadded to that enormous speed another speed which we computed to be equal to a third of that already attained.

We could not, as I said, realise this intense velocity so far beyond any terrestrial speed—even that of the ball as it leaves the cannon's mouth. Yet the knowledge of it made us doubly watchful to catch the first sign of an atmosphere, for should we continue this course uninterrupted—like a comet or falling star—we should blaze up, and either drop on the new world a blot of molten steel, or be whirled away, blasted and burnt up on a wild comet-like track—to form, perchance, a study for some latter day Venusian astronomer, as our erratic orbit brought us again and again within his ken.

When journeying between the earth and moon none of this fierce speed troubled us, the distance in itself so small (but a two hours journey at our present pace), and the fact that the speed of the moon in its orbit is the same as that of the earth's diurnal motion had greatly helped us.

This new world, too, possessed a moon, but not such a one as accompanied the earth—smaller, held by a shorter chain, and moving across the diurnal motion of the planet, while its speed was very large; it would form a curious study to a gazer on the surface of the new world.

We resolved, however, to make, if possible, some use of it, for we dreaded the many days which we should need to consume ere we could sufficiently check our headlong career, to venture into the denser air of Venus.

By creating for ourselves a temporary orbit, which should at first graze, as it were, the exterior of both orbs (viz.—Venus and its attendant moon) and afterwards gradually lessen till it was altogether included in the atmosphere of the planet, we reckoned to bring all the powers of gravitation into play, and make of them a more effectual brake than could be obtained in any other way.

Also, by bringing our course into the same plane as that of the moon, we should be able to examine it as we passed over and by it.

Indeed, we reckoned that the completion of the second circle of this orbit would bring down our speed to that of the lesser orb.

But all this while we were swiftly nearing our destination; the great globe of Venus, in apparent size far beyond that of the earthly moon, now began to grow fast upon us.

It came—that wished-for sound, like the noise of far-off wings, or the whisper of a zephyr; but thus only for a while, like a nearing cataract or coming storm it grew upon us.

Then the mighty wings of our vessel began to play, beating swiftly the thickening air, and driving us fast upward again into space, but not before a great glow of heat pervaded all the ship, growing every moment stronger, though we had now left the thicker air. "Start the cold air machine," said Moxton, "or there will be no end to this business." This soon assisted us, though the heat gathered by the steel exterior of our vessel still continued to strike inward. We were again in the depths of space borne by our own velocity, with nothing to retard, nothing to guide us. Weir, who was on the look-out, already beginning to abuse the Venusian moon, when we caught sight of it. Beautiful indeed had Moxton calculated our course; we could see it like a huge ball spinning in the shadow of the planet away before us. Our course would take us very near it; we were, perhaps, two hours ere we came to it. Then there came a sudden roar, a huge swerve of our vessel, as under its influence we shot in again to the planet. Again we repeated the experiment, although I now had the command, and Moxton in the look-out. "Keep her in it," they both said, and we dipped down so close as well nigh to touch the feathery clouds; this was enough for us all; the heat we subsisted in for the next hour would have fairly cooked any dead substance. But as we got clear again and began to cool, we saw what an immense part of our speed we had lost, we were well satisfied with the effects of our purgatorial discipline. Now, although we were sailing in a smaller circuit, we almost failed to catch again the moon.

We seemed to creep on the little satellite but inch by inch. At last, however, we drew near, helped on by its attraction as we approached it. So small was it that when it looked like *terra firma* we could observe its rotundity. We seemed to be floating, floating towards it on our back. It seemed at one time as though we should have to use our explosives to prevent our vessel being cast on her back on this airless little orb—an accident we certainly had never calculated on.

But at last we caught the welcome sound; then she heeled over, and we floated silently down on to a smooth sandy plain.

We took in a specimen of the air. It was thin and poor; scarcely sufficient to sustain the lowest forms of life, and the orb itself looked cold, dry, bare, and grey, a few meagre lichens being the only visible living things.

We prepared to strike off again, for there, hanging above us, as though it might suddenly fall and crush us into oblivion, hung the great planet, half in sunshine, half in shadow, covering a third of the sky, hanging right over our heads its clouds and waters, mountains and forests, spread out in wonderful state above us.

We would not lose time on this useless orb, so alike that it might have served as a prototype for the attendant of our own earth. We were growing familiar with new spheres, and our familiarity was working to its proverbial end.

We thought far more of our vessel than of the orb when, like a living creature, she reared herself as a tower on the plain. But as we wished to lose as much of the speed of this satellite as we could, we pointed her back towards the way she came; then gathering her power, and throwing it into a sudden and continued motion of her wings, and, opening the thunder of her artillery, she sprang away, and rushed upwards to the larger world.

For a little while we could see our rushing speed; then the little moon seemed to be leaving us, and we to be hanging out in space.

For hours we were thus, and well pleased to be so, as the passing time told plainly of the speed parted with. The planet now beneath us—for the instinct of gravity soon changed as we left the moon—was in its revolutions, bringing another face to our view, and we only needed that as we extended the air again we should bring our course into unison with the planet's diurnal motion, to reduce our speed to an earthly measure.

Once more it came—the rush of air growing to a thunderous roar; and we must steer upwards and outwards, but not afar. Still, though the seas and mountains fled away beneath us, we were able to keep within the higher atmosphere, and ever and anon to take a dip into the region of the clouds.

We were weary with watching and waiting—tired, yet determined to endure to the end of our journey ere we slept. The gallant speed and the great plunging dips which our vessel made grew monotonous to us. Below us lay a sea—well nigh an ocean. Moxton took from our stores a large electric ball, which could be discharged from a cannon and would burn with an intense light for some time afterwards. He pointed it straight down and discharged it into the ocean beneath us, we saw it strike the water and plough through the blue depths for a mile or more, then lay like a drowned sun beneath us.

"That will do," said Moxton. "Shall I take the helm?"

It was given him, and under his hands the vessel made a short turn, then with her wings set to catch the air she rushed downwards. It was a terrific plunge—perhaps seven miles as we came, but we knew our strength. How beautifully our wings closed in ere we touched the blue element. A heavy blow, a prolonged hiss and we were careering beneath the waves, but well did the elastic liquid do its work. Under the facile hand of Moxton, the *Star Climber* was already returning on her own tracks, coming nearer the dimly-lit surface and circling around in a comparatively small space.

"That will do," we said to Moxton, and almost at once, like a denizen of the deep, the *Star Climber* clove the surface of the water.

We looked out, and indeed our journey was ended—*we were floating on a calm sea*, with a great sun casting its long sloping rays upon us, a blue sky above us, and away a mile on the right was seen the cloud of steam our entrance into the water had raised. Moxton stepped to our outer cabin, closed the door—we waited while we heard the withdrawal of the air tight plugs, then his voice sang out—"All right," and Weir's hand, which had been resting on the levers, gave the motion. Our ceilings and roof, which had seemed so solid for the last four months, began to lift and throw themselves back, till we stood out on the deck—fell in the free air—a slight breeze sweeping over us, and a slight swell rising and falling along the sides of our vessel.

11

After all our troubles we were landed safe. We were floating on an ocean of another world. 'Twas not quite the same as that we left—it seemed both clearer and softer, for a long way down we could see, and for a long time saw nothing but water, then shoals of fish came round—not fish such as we have on earth—but fish of pronounced forms—fish with fins like hands—fish with elongated fins—on which we did not doubt they could walk when in a shallower water. But then stranger than all we saw them form bands, and glide past us in ranks with a leader waving his long fin-like arm, directing or beckoning them.

Now, too, we began to feel the changing atmosphere. Night was coming on—but what was night to us? We knew that all around the northern pole of the planet was spread the long six months' day, and again rising from the ocean, we swept onwards.

Two hours landed us in another climate. We got away from the forests and water out on to a vast high dreary plain, with the sun about ten degrees above the horizon.

Away to the north stretched the limitless desert, and all around us a huge waste of sand.

Here again we rested and took counsel—for nothing like human life had we seen, and not a bird in the air. We had seen troops of beasts cropping the herbage on the open ground, but had gone on wondering and hoping.

And there in this solitary place we determined to spend the night—at least our night. We put out our gangways, and descended to the ground; we walked around our vessel and looked at her closely. She was not that blue and gold and silver creation which left the other world; the cankerous mist through which we passed had spoiled her beauty, yet otherwise she was as sound as when we started in her.

It was an intense relief to stretch our limbs by walking on the solid earth. During our voyage, where a hasty step would send you flying up against the roof, and even the heaviest things were without appreciable weight, our muscles had, despite our best endeavours, become relaxed and weakened; and we found a very slight amount of exercise sufficient for us.

As we returned to our boat, Weir was, as usual, in the most frolicsome of humours, and I almost in the opposite mood.

I mentally compared myself to the seer in the Revelations—"Behold! one woe is past, and another cometh quickly." It was the thought of the coming days of solitude, when Weir and Moxton should have gone back to the world, yet not thought in its purity, but the thought debased and made painful by an understratum of want of faith in the new generation. Weir, perhaps, rightly interpreted it, when he exclaimed—"Yes, truly you will be a second Adam, but where, alas, is thy Eve? Never mind, Hope, perhaps an old cherubim may turn up to keep you company. You could lodge him in the tent, you know."

But I could not joke with him. Strange and new ideas were thronging my mind. Moxton, seeing this, brought out the real *aqua vitae*, and we drank in liquor that might have been distilled from the veins of the ancient Gods—"To the new world, and to our farther success."

'Twas a wondrous medicine—all that alcohol seems to the savage, when he feels it tingling with pleasure through all his veins, and throwing a glamour of light over his very soul.

Like alcohol, too, the excitement it caused was very great; even a strong brain would go wild with delight, and under a regime of excess, the overpowered subject seemed led as by Houries in a flowery way; seemed to rest on beds of asphodel and live in joy; the opium smokers' heaven was always his, meat and drink were no longer needed, the swiftly attenuating body seemed a cage too fragile to hold the soul which would step laughingly over the portal of death.

While, on the other hand, if used with due discretion under its glorious influences, these soft, these frail bodies of ours—if uninjured by accident, if not crushed by brute force—might outlive the very world we stood on, and who could say, perchance, even the system that this world is moving with—yea, why should we not go out with the speed of a comet on the thousand years' journey to another sun—another system.

We—Moxton, Weir and I—all believed in this elixir. Our lives were, if not supremely blest, very happy, and had we not even now solved the great problem and opened out a dwelling-place for the people of the future, we did not doubt that next generations would surpass us as much as—"Yes," I said aloud, "as much as you do me." Nor could I repress a return of that distrustful bitter feeling which seemed to well up from some unknown and longer buried spot in my heart—I had scarcely felt it since Edith Weir had given me her love.

I wished them at that moment to come over and clasp me by the hand in old world fashion, and to say that we stood or fell together, that they would be always with me.

But Moxton smiled almost in pity. "Those feelings of yours, Hope, are the strangest relics you preserve of the past. You carry fear like a devil in your heart, and every now and then he rises up and frightens you. The reign of violence is nearly done, and should the world ever weary of you and need the air you breathe for better lips, it would but be like a cry of conscience to you, never articulated or breathed through any tangible mouth or spirit, it would be no cause for fear. I am sure you could now for the good of humanity resign with a calm mind, your body to the dust." I did not answer, for they both knew my thoughts, and I think both felt a longing for those softer spirits, those kinder natures, those eyes which even now, now and again, knew tears. I know that in my heart Edith was again enshrined, chasing worlds and systems and planets far away, and filling it with herself, till my breath came quicker, and mine eyes grew bright under her influence. She was there so truly—"so near and yet so far." We looked out and saw the great sun moving round, and felt the air thin and keen, yet tempered by his beams. We took a last glance around, making all things safe; and then, for the first time since leaving our present earth, we all slept, resolving to visit together all the wonders of the new world, and to see together all that we should find.

12

The poles of the planet Venus are at such an angle that about half the planet enjoys alternately a day of three months—a long dim day of twilight, and then night; as a natural consequence, the regions approaching this country are strangely affected. When we woke in the morning we saw the first proof of this in the low sun, still hanging at the same altitude, the live-long night he had been thus creeping around. So that here there was no day or night, morning or evening, and the waste of desert around us seemed as if made for these monotonous periods.

We spread out the wings of our vessel and went on our way—but found the land still rising as we went north—and though the cold did not increase with the increasing altitude, as it would on the earth, the air grew thinner, and the barometer sank lower and lower, till it touched the fourteenth inch. Breathing became very laborious work.

We had determined to go right over the pole of the planet, but, as we did not like to shut ourselves up again, we were soon obliged by the rarefied air to turn to the lower and warmer regions, going away swiftly till grass and wood and water again began to reign, then sailing slowly, and not too high, that we might observe if anything like humanity should appear. We saw troops of beasts, four-legged and two-legged ape-like creatures, kangaroo, or more properly three-legged animals; but none of them seemed struck with wonder as we glided slowly above them. They all fed and played and fought, as though there were nothing new under their Heaven, and if we swept down near them went away with screams and cries to their shelters. Their forms were very strange, ever recalling something we knew, yet always differing from it; yet what we most noticed—what seemed to be an unvarying characteristic—was that, whether large or small, they all moved in troops and bands, all fed and fought together, and all seemed well provided for either attack or defence; but nothing human appeared, nought of a nature similar to our own.

I can hardly tell how much we wished—how our hearts would have gone out towards any living creature which should have risen above the level of the animal world, or how our thoughts wondered over the intellectual union which might arise, should two such experiences join their pleasures, their results; yet here there was enough to recall the wildest wandering thoughts, as we went hither and thither to and from every new object, everything that promised a revelation, over lakes and mountains, rivers and forests, till we felt ourselves in the tropical regions, with the high sun blazing overhead, and the great bush herbage, and vast trees all about us.

Yet none of this would please Moxton. He would press on to the winter half of the planet, to the land of shadow, and we expected of ice and snow, for warm as the planet was, we thought that three months' exclusion from the sun's heat, would bring the temperature very low. Yet we could not help lingering, turning to each new beauty of flower and fruit, leaf, or herbage, skimming near the edge of the forest, or the waters of the rivers, hoping to see some new elephant or huge mastodon. For the appetite for the wonderful, not sufficiently substantial I suppose, for Solomon's classification is, however, one of the hardest things to satisfy, so far from ever crying enough, it grows with its food.

So we were borne steadily onward through the fresh air of the new world—were always eager to behold something fresh—unsatisfied with the wonders of Heaven. We seemed to forget the leagues that we had travelled, unmindful of our great fate, to run like older babes in the wood from flower to flower as fancy guided us.

Yet stopping often as we did, our immense speed led us fast from clime to clime, and before the natural day would decline the sun began to grow low on the northern horizon; the tropical forests to be replaced by grassy plains and rolling, scantily timbered hills. Sometimes, too, we came on arid sand—huge dry deserts without even the proverbial vulture to enliven them; then succeeded strange twilight, with the sun low down, and its beams striking along the world. The air seemed to grow vague and yellow, a thickness and fogginess pervaded everything. How changed seemed the vegetation—rotting leaves and bare boughs; huge stalked grass, half-decayed—and here, too, we saw more birds, great downy owls, and bats to which the devil of the middle ages was a mild creature. It also seemed the land of frogs and toads—huge speckled tawny creatures, not good to look at; and the vegetation altered fast now, the reign of the fungus seemed to have begun. The ground, the trees, the water were covered with minute forms, and in the opener spaces huge growths stranger than the cactus or fungus of the world, immense groups of all shapes, so strange were they, that even Moxton agreed to come to a stand for a while.

We left our vessel and walked among these wonders—taking, however, our weapons with us—we seemed like the little men of Gustave Doré, walking in some strange ante-diluvian world. Now they rose around us like the groups of miniature towers with their snow-white tops and their flesh-coloured interiors; others would strike away in convolutions over yards of ground in disgusting mimicry of a dissected animal; others built up of narrow ridges and spines, and every interesting shape, and every shade and colour—some beautiful, some hideous. One large flower-like thing, like a thick-lipped convolvulus, had attracted us, and Moxton thrust his stick into it. Its anthers closed immediately on it, then its thick leaves folded down with a wonderful grip. But if Moxton was the first to be surprised, the would-be glutton was the next. With scarcely any visible motion beyond the setting of his muscles, he set the magnetic power of which he had a wonderful command, thrilling into the flabby monster. The effect was instantaneous, it curled for a moment as under galvanic action, then its whole system collapsed and seemed to fall into itself in flaccid weakness, while its juices exhaled and dripped from its whole surface.

Perhaps had we seen these things under the broad sunlight, they would have made like impression, but the strange light, the long shadows, and the great patches of colour, the result of minute organism, covering both earth and water, made them strange and wonderful to look on, like a peep show of Dame Nature; but it was not good to stay in, and our curiosity being satisfied, there was nothing to keep us.

We went to the *Star Climber*, which seemed more like a home than it had been for months past, and we felt quite a pleasure as we trod once again the familiar deck. We passed on over miles and miles of this twilight country, the sun going lower and lower till every little hollow was in perpetual shade, and there seemed no end to the shadow of a tree. We had still our decks open, and could perceive the chilling temperature. This did not seem the region of storms, but an unaltering, unrelieved, steady rawness gradually verging into a pronounced state of cold. It was many hundred miles before we came to the real ice and snow, where the water was all locked up, and all the ground covered with the downy mantle. But here again we saw occasionally troops of beasts dashing away in the dim light, and a solitary large-eyed bird rose and flitted into the darkness that spread around us. The stars were very faint, the air did not seem yet to be clear of the mist and lingering sunshine, and there above us—a dim star amongst thousands—lay the earth, our native home; and as we looked at it the thought that we should soon stand there again seemed to partake of impossibility and madness.

Weir said, "I wish you would not think so dismally, Hope; those ideas of yours would unstring the nerves of a lion. There is nothing renders a man so helpless as that sense of fatality and impossibility."

Moxton said with a laugh, "I should think it would be less trouble for you to rule against the entrance of Hope's ideas than for him to perfectly control them."

This brought a smile to our faces, though from different feelings. Weir was always kind-natured. My smile was, I suppose, so grim that Moxton, looking at me, said, "Well?"

I answered, "I do not care what either of you think when I feel like this."

"No," replied Moxton, "the human brain was so dulled and attuned to sorrow through many centuries, that the sentiment of it is bound to be pleasant, wakening as it does all the half forgotten motions. 'Tis the same in kind as that the old athlete feels after years of disuse he stretches his muscles again."

But it was growing cold. We agreed to again shut down the outer covering of the *Star Climber*, as Moxton wished to run through this region of darkness, and as we sped on our way it grew brighter, the air seemed clearer, the ground sparkled with snow and frost; the rivers and seas were coated with ice, a thorough winter reigned all around us.

Volume

13

PREPARING TO START—SUSPICIOUS THOUGHTS

From fruit to flower—from the deep dale to the treeladen forest—from mountain to sea—from rivers of bright water to the desert ground—we wandered and searched, like children on a holiday, ever eager to see, to know, and to discover, and perhaps I, John Hope, secretly feared to meet that hour when Moxton and Weir would leave me alone on the planet and again tempt the dangers of the great deep.

But the dreaded hour ever comes swiftly; pleasure makes wings for time, and but for memory it would be worth while to follow life's trail through the desert of existence for all the golden hours and bright oases which we can see; but memory—memory gives again and again each happy thought, each celestial moment thrills its thousand times through all our heart, brightening life's dullest hours.

So, now our holiday was past, why in truth, with so great a deed accomplished, should Weir and Moxton longer stay? Everything that I could want for years to come was stored in my little castle, which, though small, was yet formidable in its powers of defence, and in the journeyings, which day by day we accomplished, nothing had we seen capable of hurting man, or in any way coping with his sure and terrible arms. There were, indeed, huge lion-like animals which moved under leaders, and worked together like an army, but they never left their native forest, and these seemed the most formidable, roaming without check through a large part of the world.

We had selected a spot some hundreds of feet above the common level, for here all the water seemed land-locked, standing like inland lakes at all sorts of heights, rising and falling, with the seasons, and with no general inter-communication. It was a fine sweeping plain within the tropics, but kept cool by its elevation, and by the fact that on the still higher ground spread a large lake. There were a few trees scattered here and there, sometimes in clumps, sometimes almost deepening into a coppice, and under a near group I had a large tent fixed for comfort in the warmer weather.

Yet, despite the want of apparent danger, and the complete reign of brute strength, there was in all our minds a strange dread and uneasiness at parting, and indeed we surely needed to leave a large margin for possibilities in reckoning the coming years, for should aught happen on their homeward voyage, might they not be whirled away on their unprecedented course till they became but a mite of senseless matter gripped in the undying hand of fate; and who then should be mourned—they or I, a solitary being in a lonely world? Yes, I might for ages carry on that awful existence; I felt even as though it had already begun, hoping from long year to year that another vessel would tempt that wondrous deep from which no travellers had as yet returned—hoping—but ah! how vainly—hoping to see again those glorious beings which woke me from my wondrous sleep; hoping—ah! hope is never the word for that infinite yearning—to see her but again—it seemed worth a century of life—to hear those gentle words, to feel the least breath of that love which was beyond all pity or compassion.

Moxton, and her brother, too, their hearts seemed clouded and confused to me, and the sleeping devil which had seemed to live beneath Moxton glared as when I first knew him, returning like a dream to trouble my brain, and with it many fearful thoughts. For was not I an alien, an outcast, and had not I presumed to wed myself to the future in defiance of fate and law? Then, as I had done so much—led the van in the battle of force against brute matter—had not this people, this council of nations, carried out well their unwritten commandments, and given me by my own choice their highest sepulchre, their widest tomb?

The men, too, whom I had chosen, or who had chosen me—was there not a fitness—her brother, who would have been wronged in his sister's union—and Moxton, did not her image dwell deep in his heart? aye, deeper perhaps than I could fathom—by the world judged, by my own conscience condemned—and these two men, though I believed they loved me as brothers—my fitting executioners? Yes, what kind cruelty! I could wander at large in my tomb; I could live till time itself grew gray, yet could never again mingle with the perfection of the future, or see the wondrous light in those faces now lost to me. Yes, this was why they lingered, and walked apart; why a cloud had settled over those great spirits which I was but beginning to leave.

I was sitting and thinking in my lonely castle, the *Star Climber* lay resting on the ground some hundreds of yards away, and I saw Weir and Moxton returning through the lengthening shadows. I could but fancy their minds, but in fuller comradeship than I had ever known with them; yet, as they grew nearer, that tide of unhappy thought went back, a stronger manhood seemed to be asserting itself, till it was as though my brain—so long ago benumbed in that wondrous sleep—was but awakening; as though the delicate fibres of sense had been so near dissolution, perhaps even touched with decay in those long dead years, that a horror as of death was always hanging over me, breeding fearful thoughts and strange fancies. Yes, I had known of one such unhappy case, where death had actually been, yet was the great conqueror driven out; the miserable man had died from bad air in some earth shaft, had been pronounced dead, and given over for burial, and so taken charge of by the savants of science, and after many hours had elapsed, revivified. But then the trouble began; he was not himself in the finer tissues within the brain, corruption had begun, and a terrible fear and horror always hung over him—more especially as regarded his friends. It was a fearful drama when his sons saw the once dead man again—himself, yet not himself, with the taint and fear of death always upon him. His recovery had not been made known to them, and it was only the strange instinct which drew—yet frightened—drew him by an awful fascination to his natal spot, that brought about the discovery and made the fact known to the world.

By this time Moxton and Weir were drawing nigh, and could not but move uneasily under all that sense of thought. They must have divined afar off all that tempestuous feeling, for Weir came, and laying his hand on my shoulder, said—"I shall bring back my sister, Hope, as surely as I reach the earth; those thoughts that trouble you are, as you know, but a nightmare, as far from the truth as from your latter self."

And Moxton, looking at me with a face that would have made doubt die of shame, said—"If I liked the girl as much as you do, Hope, I would send her to you and seek to find some other, because I know how much she likes you. You must not think because once her image dwelt awhile in my mind no other can grow there. I think there are thousands whom you would have loved had they been brought near you, and you know our present lives have wider instincts, and are more in unison with all nature and one another."

They both knew better than I could tell them that all these thoughts were but as dreams, though fated perhaps to be dreamt during the night of their departure, and only to be thoroughly done away by the morn of their re-coming.

The few last days came swiftly. We all collected fruits, flowers, and the smaller animals, to be taken back. There was not much in the way of utility, but for beauty, variety, strangeness—both beast and bird, fruit and flower, were endless.

The new air of the planet conspired to give life and vivacity to every act, and because we liked these days they seemed the faster to flee away, for both Moxton and Weir dreaded the months of monotony to come. Almost a fear seemed to hang over them as the hour of departure drew nigh—not for themselves, but for me.

"There is no doubt we were fools," said Weir, "to arrange to leave you here. There [could be] many things on this planet of which we know nothing—even the beasts have almost sense enough to besiege you. If I were you I should not travel except in the air. You are quite safe in that little boat, and even when you are about here I would always keep my revolver in my hand—make a habit of it. I don't know what we would do if, when we came back, we found anything wrong with you; it would spoil the spirit of the whole enterprise; to us it would hardly be a success. I think there are animals we have not seen, four-footed men, perhaps, as cunning and as cruel as the most ancient savage. There is certainly not much to attract anything here except grass-feeders, but you know the grass-feeders are themselves food."

I promised duly to take care of myself, and, indeed, intended to do so, for life was dear to me as ever.

Early morning was the time appointed for their leavetaking; then the planet would bring us round to the appointed place, and the *Star Climber* once more dash away on her heavenly route.

We spent a large part of the night in preparing for the start, this needing nice calculation and accurate despatch; for although if they once came into the limits of the earth's attraction their erratic orbit and natural motion would bring them into the atmosphere, and so enable them to land, yet, were they so far out as to miss the short circle, then, indeed, God knows whither they might wander. Might they not, like other lost travellers, lose not only the way but the sense to re-find it, and if not stopped by one of the outer planets, go out into an abyss more dread than that of the dyspeptic's dream? But these were all foolish visions, founded on nought, for we were dealing with real facts and certainties, and not more surely have summer and winter, and day and night, followed without alteration or accident, than that if started truly on our course we should follow it and arrive at its end. We had, however, decided to start the *Star Climber* by a different method. Instead of circling round to attain speed, and then going in the direction as the ship moved outwards towards space by steering or wing power, Moxton determined to poise the *Star Climber* in the air, keeping her steady and motionless with her lesser vibratory motion, till, like a rifle or telescope, she was accurately sighted, then discharge, as we had done in the Magellan cloud, our rearward artillery—this would give her a swift and true start, with about three times the speed with which we left the earth; besides which, they would still have the ten miles of atmosphere to correct any slight error, and all their wing power to accelerate their already swift motion.

DREAM—NEW INHABITANTS

The broad sun was throwing his misty beams over the dew-laden planet. We had shaken hands; we had parted. I stood on the grassy turf, Moxton and Weir on the flying vessel. "Once more, Weir, good-bye! good-bye!" Stern time never yet tarried. With waving hands and lingering looks they were gone. The huge lids of the vessel that had till now lain open, began to rise and slowly fold them within their air-tight clasp. Weir appeared again for a moment at the lesser door, then that, too, was closed, and for an instant all was silent. Then the long wings stretched themselves out and began to move with a short, rapid motion, quickening, till the grass and herbs beneath were beaten from the ground by the fiercely-driven air, and as those wing points grew into a blue haze the grand vessel lifted herself up, steadily moving away from me till well nigh a mile distant.

I did not wish to be left stunned with the noise of her departure. Again I saw her poise herself steadily. Gradually the fore part rose from the level plane till the vessel hung steadily at an acute angle with the planet's surface. This, as in their start from the earth, would give some twelve miles of pretty dense atmosphere to travel in before the thinner air was reached. I knew the minute was drawing near. I saw the ship move slightly, and then seem fixed like a falling tower across the firmament without even a tremble or perceptible quiver.

Then, at the appointed second, the stream of fire flashed out and the fearful deafening roar fell on my ear. I saw her rush, upwards, onwards, amid such a continuous thunder peal as this world certainly never heard before; like the evil angels of old, she left in fire and flame. Swift, like a gigantic meteor, she fled away; she hung for some seconds out over the horizon, then grew smaller and smaller, till like a point of light—a star—she vanished, and I—with half my dreams, half my hopes realised—stood alone on the new planet. Alone. Yes; though we had been here weeks, how strange the grass, how new each leaf! Each little unfamiliar flower lifted its eye to mine as though some angel whispered in its ear that I was alone, and it feared and wondered at me.

Then I sank down on the grass and cried like a child, like a woman who knows the vanity, the sweetness of grief. I hid my face on the earth, although there was no eye to see. Then I grew calm. I recollect the breeze playing about my head, the warm sun striking down on me. Then consciousness faded—I wandered into the land of dreams, and there again I lay stretched, but out on a burning plain, an unutterable desert. I rise up; I look abroad, and there before me in the uncertain distance some thing with two colourless insect-like wings stood stiffly up, still as if dead, and still farther away another, and another. Measureless distance all around. Like dead infernal things do my thoughts speak them; and ere ever you come near them they rise and move away; and their wings have no motion; then stand again, still, silent, horribly certain. Is it a remnant of an unknown hell left here, where forgotten of all, unseen in the array of the eternal ages, they are tormented not; they wander no more, but flit, flit from all and stay here for ever? Then that grim vision faded, and a voice cried—"Herein is the prophecy—that thou should'st work among rotten wood, having an ass's tail for a sky scraper, and wanting both wit and money." I grew puzzled and confused; conscious again of the hot sun striking on me; then dimly, yet ever increasing with my returning senses, a second consciousness of some other presence, aye, no foot on the sand, but of beings standing over me—gods or angels, men or devils, what or who? The sense of their presence wrenched back my senses from the world of the brain's play-time, and brought at last to me the uses of my mortal vision. Strange beings! how shall I describe them? with no likeness to humanity except that they stood on two legs; with arms, yet not arms; faces human, yet how unlike!

I woke to the sense of their presence, to see them gazing down, arms linked to each other, male and female, gazing with soft eyes on my yet recumbent figure, their fine bodies covered with a down—neither of bird nor animal—soft and dark, and their heavy, lithe limbs, such as might have developed from that earliest of prehistoric elephant, had not the heat of a younger world debased him, and nature's giant youth pushed him in her recklessness to balk rather than serve.

They did not move as I awakened; they stood still as I leaned on my elbow, too crazed with wonder to speak, as drawn up by fascination I arose. I even advanced towards them. Then the smaller one shrank back, while the other lifted a limb into the air; but I spread out my two hands and I think my lips made unintelligible attempts to speak, but whether any words broke from them I do not know. I think my speech then dwindled into unintelligible mumblings, like those of an idiot, but the action was understood. Strange sounds they made; the huge limb descended; it touched my hands with a soft motion; then I stroked that extended arm; and impelled by those independent workings of the brain, I became emboldened and took the quaint ending of that limb in my hand, and shook it as I would a friend's hand. Then what was the laughter of the planet broke in motion over their faces, and moved in the air with a refreshing, peace-giving breath. It swept away my dread—a smile broke on my features—I went still nearer—I put an arm on each and laid my face against the face of the smaller one. Each motion of confidence was reciprocated; she inclined to me, touching me with a soft motion. Then we parted, and again looked at each other.

How strange it seemed—we could not speak. There was intelligence, knowledge, in every line of their features, and with low, strange voices they turned to each other and seemed to converse. "Will you come with me?" I said, and I think it was the first intelligible sentence I had uttered since I saw them. But as with assenting motions, and a low, sweet intonation that sounded to me like a repetition of my own words "come! come!" they turned to me. I led the way to my castle.

They would not enter. They stood a few yards from the door with their arms again linked around each other, and I could but think they were wise to use such prudence. I brought out of my stores what I could think of to please the eye or delight the palate. I spread these things on the grass and sat down beside them, beckoning them to do the same, and to eat and drink with me. They did this without fear, but so daintily and so delicately that I could but wonder how they supported life in those strong muscular bodies. Their little attentions to each other—like two lovers, or still more like two children playing at a feast—were so new and original, that I was occupied with but watching them. These were not savages, and how far removed from animals—over and above each kindly motion, each laughter-loving thought lit their eyes; how much sagacity they had needed to keep themselves hidden from our strange invasion, and how much courage to come so near to me when my companions left in such a chariot of fire and noise I could scarcely tell. Perhaps they had watched us day by day—had seen that cruelty and destruction were not the gods of our nature. I tried hard to begin to learn their words or signs, or to teach them mine, but each feature, each bone, each muscle was different, and I saw that it would be a work of time ere we could begin to form sounds which could be called imitation. When we rose up, they in their turn beckoned me, and I followed, or, rather, went with them; not, however, carelessly. I provided myself, besides the arms I always carried, with another revolver, whose explosive bullets would blow up a rhinoceros. I never needed them. Afterwards I thought almost with shame at my doubts concerning my gentle companions. They led me on, keeping up an occasional converse, beckoning and pointing often to me, but in such a way that I did not understand.

They led me to the borders of the upland lake, and there under the tall herbage was a rude boat, or rather raft. They evidently wished me to embark with them, but to this I would not consent, and after a while they left me, promising, as far as signs could point, to return again.

15

FURTHER DESCRIBES THE INHABITANTS

I walked slowly back to my dwelling, drinking in the new ideas that had come with such a flood upon me, at every step.

More than the new world to me were these creatures, more than my long sleep and awakening, more than aught save those I had left on the earth. All through the evening and night were there strange figures and quaint patient faces reliving ["relimning" in the original] themselves again and again in my brain, till all this burden of knowledge and new experience seemed almost too much for me; these older memories should have been beneath the daisies, and younger heads and happier hearts have been unravelling these mysteries, but nature's great balm of sleep comes to us alike in palace and dungeon, lying near by to many friends, or in a world alone. It came to me in my lonely castle, deep and peaceful; nor did I wake till morning light.

Bright sunshine and dewy grass greeted me as I went out, and my thoughts turned at once to my companions of yesterday—to this new race. What should I call them? By what name should I think of them? Ah! how poorly I played the part of a second Adam in this new world. He named all the creatures, and I could not find a name for the first of them. But, then I thought of the star, the planet of love, and determined to call them by it, namely, Venus, and by that name they were afterwards known.

Scarcely need to say that I looked around to see if I could discover anywhere those quaint figures, or that I listened if I might catch the low murmurings of the Venus tongue, but nought could I see or hear of them. So I returned and rolled out my little boat, determined to find them.

My boat—the *Midge* she was called, and, perhaps, in the world I had left, never was there constructed a greater triumph of mechanical skill and beauty—as fair as a lady's finger, as glorious as an angel among the birds, by land, or air, or water. She could run, or fly, or swim. I got on board of her and took a preliminary canter through the fresh air, speeding on till the rushing wind seemed to take away my breath. Then I returned, closed up my castle, and went to seek the Venuses.

I was not long in reaching the upland lake on which they had launched; it stretched away large and clear before me, with long arms like bands of bright water running far up between the hills. But 'twas as calm and as lifeless as when, with Moxton and Weir, I had passed over it. The sedge and herbage were untrampled on the bank, and the fish sped away at my shadow. But I never doubted the Venuses would come. I never for an instant thought my vision of yesterday was a dream. I dropped down with the *Midge* contentedly into the water, watching the finny inhabitants of the deep, waiting contentedly in the morning sunshine. Nor had I long to wait, for soon upon one of the long, winding waves of water I saw them appearing, seemingly just starting on their day's voyage. I put the *Midge* in motion, and soon came near them.

How strange they looked! how uncouth to the eye now freed from excitement, yet not trained by familiarity, each with a rude paddle propelling the boat! But as they came near they shipped their oars, and began to greet me with bows and waving of the hands, with ununderstood, yet soft and pleasant voices.

"The Venuses." I kept repeating to myself the word each time I looked at them, as though it could in a manner explain their identity to me, or help me to class them among the beings I had known—but as Venuses, as new and strange beings, must they ever remain. This is what I seemed to be learning during my first interview with them.

With their consent I tied their raft to the *Midge*, and under their guidance we went back to find their home. Nor could I be sure what I should find, whether camp, or village, or solitary hut, but from their signs guessed the latter. Yet it could not be that they were enacting Eden in another world; they must surely have some cousins or aunts, or at least must have had a father or a mother. But presently, as we went farther up the fiord-like water, their solitary hut or nest appeared built on piles—out in the water, covered with grass and boughs, and only to be approached by coming along a row of stilt-like piles driven between it and the land.

We tied the boats to the posts and they invited me to enter. 'Twas a small mossy cabin, with a strange, bird-like air pervading it, but scrupulously clean, neat, and almost pretty, as if half a bird's instinct had been by some beneficent power bequeathed to them, but so small that, apart from the space occupied by the fruits and nuts which they had in store, there was hardly room for them to stretch themselves.

But were they indeed so completely alone? I thought and asked, as I looked out again and could see no sign of other habitations.

Was theirs indeed a semi-solitary existence? I could hardly think so while their low voices and pleasant laughter murmured and rippled in my ears. Yet, by signs, I gathered in reply that they were truly now alone—all others far away; and as I looked at their provisions I divined the reason—if they lived without tillage on the fruits of the ground, they must need be few in number, and live far apart.

I ate of their provision, and from their motions, and as yet incomprehensible voices, began to see dimly new facts, which afterwards grew real and trustworthy.

Yet, after all, it was they who had to learn. Their mind in its best phases had little that was superior to humanity. Some happier thoughts—some sweet companionship—some feelings of freedom and pleasure—new perhaps to any inhabitant of my native world; yet of that great body of thought which has arisen from our mechanical and omniverous propensities, they knew nothing, and as I afterwards found out, were saved from stupidity and savageness by the long-continuing slowness of their mental emotions, and by their wonderful care of, and kindness to, each other.

We walked by their own way to the shore near us, and there I showed the Venuses the mystery of fire, and they were sufficiently civilised to wonder at and not worship it. They fed it with dry boughs, and hovered around it until I drew them away, that I might teach them the further wonders of fishing and cooking—not, indeed, those gaunt things like swimming bats or submarine devils which I had first seen when with Moxton and Weir, which seemed to go out in troops and move in squadrons like sensitive beings, but fine, scaly things with large swelling shoulders, and whose brain frame would scarce hold your little finger, and which jumped in ecstasy on a gaudy fly, and afterwards were led captives at will by a thread of silk. They evidently appreciated grilled-fish and fire, and would soon, I saw, be as completely civilised in these respects as the inhabitants of the earth.

Yes, my thoughts had already left my old home, and were clustering round these new creatures, thinking for them and of them whilst I knew the *Star Climber* was rushing through space with Weir and Moxton, and that millions awaited its coming with every variety of hope and fear; and that sweet girl-mind, so full of wisdom and innocence, which had entered into companionship with mine and glorified it—and not it only, but to me all the future—was an eddy in the rising tide of thought. And these new creatures—I almost laughed as I looked at them—yet when they fanned their faces and gazed on me their idea again resumed its sway, their weight of individuality and character did away with the feeling of the grotesque which now and then began to rise up, and prompt me to surname them "The Happy Ogres," and dance around them like an unmitigated lunatic.

I think it must have been the overweight of thought—too much done, too much seen—for sometimes broke on me an awful desire, for sheer stupidity, to toss all thought and wisdom to the wind, and be a fool once more.

Driven by some such thought as this, I laughed right out as I looked on them, and then turned away and walked around them, as they sat on the bank of the lake watching the flickering sparks of the expiring fire, then came back and laughed again, and after that hardly felt safe from a wild spirit of facetious mockery and mimicry.

Yes, God knows the situation was thought-giving enough to an onlooker from the outer Heaven—the yellow sand, the broad sun, the two Venuses, dark and soft-furred, watching the expiring glow of the burnt wood. Great Nature's blessed peace lay on the woods and waters, and in the sunny air; yet they heeded it not, thought not of it—their hollow hands and soft bodies dabbled in the local warmth, all their thoughts intent and rapt amid the promethean spark. Nor did I, John Bentford [*sic*] Hope, care at all for Nature's beauty, though I saw and felt it—striding up and down on the hard sand, as careless of them or their thoughts as of the peace of nature—striding up and down by them, till I laughed aloud as one in madness at what I knew not, except that all things jarred and frayed, and roughened all my spirit, and the Venuses sat on without turning a thought or eye towards me or my wild motions.

16

WEIR AND MOXTON ARE STAYED ON THEIR WAY BY A METEOR

When Moxton and Weir left the planet Venus to reach once more the planet Earth they had a far longer journey before them than the previous one. They might, indeed, by waiting, have been borne into a corresponding position, but, with such an end accomplished, who would wait? Moreover, their greater speed would render their longer journey shorter in time, and as easily accomplished. There was no greater danger in the new route than the old, in both alike they might meet with wandering fragments—parts, yet outlaws, of the solar system—dangerous indeed for travellers. Yet, unlike those roving denizens of the old world, their danger did not increase with their size; when beyond a certain bulk their powers of gravity would prevent a collision.

In our first journey no meteor had rushed past us, nor had we been conscious of being touched by any mass, which was better than we expected, for, considering the immense number of small bodies that hourly fall to the earth, we thought—despite our lack of that all-potent attraction, gravity—that some stray fragment might dash itself to pieces on our sides, or pierce them like a cannon ball. So with greater confidence had Moxton and Weir set out on their homeward journey, and as they sped away their thoughts naturally turned backward to their friend left alone.

"Do you know? I pity him," said Weir, "with all he has done, and is likely to do, and we might say to be—still I pity him."

"Your pity need not be deep," answered Moxton, "take it farther back to those earlier discoverers—to Galileo and Columbus—and then Hope belongs to an older world, yet is one of this, and although he can never have the full confidence of fellowship which most of us enjoy, he has all the bright, social pleasures of companionship, and when Edith reaches him in his new world, time will not be dreary."

"Perhaps not," answered Weir, "yet I still say I pity him. I know it is something like pitying Romeo and Juliet; we would like to be one of them all the time. But just cast your thoughts back to John Hope on the planet, and then guess his thoughts from what they were before we left; he cannot help suspicion and dread; and I don't know, but I should not wonder at the frightful monotony of his life growing strong enough to bewilder his brain."

"You forget how much he has seen, and known, and even his fears and despairs are not much like monotony; besides, he may make some new discovery as startling as the two last."

"Which is the second?" asked Weir.

"Why, the road to the new world," answered Moxton.

"Yes, it does seem wonderful that after a man has outlived several generations, and taken such an acknowledged place in the world, he should elect to go on this wild voyage, and to stay on the other planet. But, at the same time, I think he is out of the road of discoveries now. What else is there to discover?"

"You might have said that at any time in the world's history. Anyhow, he might find some reasonable inhabitants, and gain something from their experience."

"I think he would be more likely to find a reasonable animal. We did not see any signs of civilization except among the fishes. Yes; that is an idea. The towns and cities may be at the bottom of the sea, and Hope can employ his spare hours in finding out something that shall enable us to walk beneath the water without putting out our cigars. Yes, I can see something left for the future generations."

"Yes," answered Moxton, "look at the instruments and see how we are going."

"I will look, my good fellow," answered Weir, "but as you know, we with all our speed are ourselves the instrument obedient to every breath or atom that stirs in space; if they move we all move with them."

"I know," answered Moxton. "They have been completely stationary, but if you noticed, as we approached any object, there was a slight tremor about it, quite discernible."

"Yes, just as there is now," answered Weir, who was gazing on the delicate hands, just, perhaps, a shade paler than usual.

The mounting of nine days was as yet the account of their voyage, since the planet lay behind them, large and lustrous, and grew from an immense orb into a broad-faced horned moon, that hung far away behind them in the purple heaven, and their course had as yet been as steady as that of the sun in the heaven.

"Just as they do now," Weir had answered, and his face did most assuredly grow pale, and the spasm of fear, given and communicated, reached and spread round Moxton's soul. Their former voyage had given them too much confidence, that broad interstellar way had as yet no aërial lighthouse, no heavenly buoy, nought to mark or guide them from danger or death.

The million worlds and the myriad aërialites chased, and crossed, and followed each other in a tangled web, an endless range of contradictory figures, all scattered abroad in the great ocean of ether through which the *Star Climber* was ever rushing, "just as they do now," said Weir, and a real, a substantial shadow fell suddenly on them, the sunlight was blotted out. Each previous half-hour had their eyes—and then better eyes, their powerful glasses—swept all around the horizon; but behind them, the country from which they sped so swiftly, on that they had seldom looked; and from right above them or from beneath, might not a fierce meteor have been long rushing? Ah, they thought so now! Vast was the speed of the *Star Climber*, but might not some erratic fragment have a speed still vastly greater—hurled from the bosom of a monstrous volcano, whose pent-up pressure had consolidated diamonds, like mountains, and whose terrific discharge should leave the shattered ruby masses like an avalanche of loosened rock, and hurl outward fragments, large as little worlds, flying with all the speed of the parent orb, and all the mighty volcanic impetus superadded? Moxton and Weir thought of this now; to each other each one's thoughts were visible, and the great shadow was over them.

Shall we blame them, that they at this moment forgot the lessons of their previous voyages, forgot that omnipotent factor, gravity?—Forgot that it had [for] some time ceased to keep up his steady pull on them and their belongings?

Shall we blame them that, springing as they thought to their posts of observation, they forgot their muscular power, and went with a bang against the ceiling, bounding and rebounding between that and the floor in dire and scrambling disorder? Shall we count the many seconds that passed ere their eyes could give tangibility to their fears? Ah! no, for in that latest instant as their glance sped outward, their hands turned to their instruments. But, ah! even then their fate was upon them.

17

J. B. HOPE ON THE PLANET

Hope left the two Venuses still on the beach, and sailed out in his boat on the lake down the long winding-like water. He did not care to return to his castle. The sight of their companionship awoke many memories of the world he had left. To have seen those two beings in their nest of moss and grasses, to hear the soft, low murmur of their voices as they seemingly grew quite unconscious of any onlooker, in their soft and lover-like play together! A gnawing sense of discontent had grown up in Hope's heart and he stayed with them no longer.

What was his life now? What was it worth, weighed in the balance of chance and fate? Those two beings, with scarcely a tenth of his knowledge, with scarcely a thought beyond themselves, were happier than he. What had it given him, all those far-reaching yearnings and strivings? What was the future to him, cut off by such an unfathomable ocean from that which had grown as dear as the light of heaven to his heart? He, whom a senseless wandering meteorite might exile for how long!—Ah, who could tell!—till he were trebly an outcast, till here, in this savage world, he grew to be as a beast among men. Yes; what were all his hopes and aspirations, his passion for progress, but the baits and bribes of the great source of life? Yes, and was not all the world drawn on like baby children, tempted by a present pleasure to fulfil an end of which they never thought?

Yes; we may flatter ourselves that we are gods—but why do we work and strive? That the life that grows up in aftertime may be moved, and pleased, and hallowed? No! but to fulfil an unsatisfied yearning that drives us remorselessly onwards, with as little thought of the end, the effect, as has the basest criminal giving way to his brute instincts. Truly, providence uses us very ill. Must we for ever toil on in the dark; must we be always as babies, coaxed with sugar plums? If life be so good, worth so much contrivance to keep alive, why cannot we grasp the Godlike end and pleasure, to fulfil which all these liquorice baits are held before our eyes? And why does the taste of pleasure beget in the nascent soul such a transformation and make each one follow the enchanter in wild route? Yes, providence takes us at the lowest valuation, and do we imagine it is wrong? Let us enjoy ourselves as we are, and trust to the hands that stretch out from bright clouds to guide us onward!

John Bentford Hope was moving steadily across the bright water. His boat, brighter than that of the poet's fancy, sped on—not drawn by some unknown current, but impelled by the same silent, tireless power which could lift it up into the air and drive it along like a bird in the sunbeams. The boat sped on; the long, watery winding way was passed, and the open lake, with a rippling breeze, was before him. Hope stayed the machinery; the boat glided slowly; then he took a pair of sculls for the boat's sides and began to drive himself through the water.

For more than an hour he pulled; then resting and looking back, saw that he was not half way. But what of that? 'Twas not to cover space that he unshipped his oars. The swift blood pulsating through his veins seemed to have swept each deluding lie from his brain. He saw the great sun sinking in peace, his own shadow stealing out on the water; the light wind dropped, and all the sweet pleasures of a summer evening stole over the planet. One cannot always see visions and dream dreams, or, what is still better, see and know that which is more strange than a vision, more wonderful than a dream. No; but lapped in the soft air, with the water gently laving the sides of his boat, he could enjoy the peace and rest of nature; assimilate the wonders he had known, and wait for the coming hours with a bright hope. Yes; till all those glad faces should look again on him—till here, too, should reign the works of man, and this planet should teem with human pleasure. Then his boat, as if impelled by a similar thought, spread out its wings, and the *Midge* seemed, with a visible tremor, to long to dash away into space, to get nearer their native country.

Later in the evening, when Hope, like a giant of old retreated into his castle, letting fall the portcullis, and barring his windows, he began to think again of the two beings he had left.

How strangely had his thought and estimate of them altered since he saw them standing over him as he awoke from his dreams! Then they were angels or devils, satyrs or fawns, something more wonderful than man. How his heart throbbed at their touch, their gentle speech and manner hallowed them in his mind. And now it was reversed—far away were the gods and goddesses of divine and beautiful stature, of noble and great mind, of power and of beauty. "Yet," said J. B. Hope to his soul, "this is but the tide of emotion, and should my comrades be delayed on their voyage how much will this new race be to me? Does not a man forget his home and his friends for a dead and lifeless thing, for an invention, for a picture, for an idea new to art and science, and will not another race—a race not human, yet having those attributes which we conceive in themselves to be the essence of humanity—fill my mind and occupy my thoughts; yes, and despite their want of mechanical culture, take a high place in the temple of my spirit, where the image of each one I have ever known is set up in its appointed niche, and seldom moved from its first estate, though, perchance, often taken down and weighed in a more perfect balance? So will these two presently gain their rightful position. What shall I call each of them?"

Then he thought of their softness, their strength, their helplessness before the dictates of fate, and joining the outcome of thoughts past and present, he named them Philomenia and Hyperion, and resolved to teach them these titles even as he would learn their own names as soon as he could master their most strange speech. Would they not soon learn to trust him; in a few days ride with him in the *Midge* to the bounds of the world; show him their friends; and would he not learn as much as they knew themselves of their past history? And what might there not be in that land of mist and darkness, where for long months the wind never came, where a grey twilight fell always, and all nature under its influence seemed to grow strange and monstrous? They had traversed it in the *Star Climber*, they had walked about in its dim labyrinths, yet had seen, they knew, but spots; and then would not any living creature have fled from the coming of their vessel, as with its wondrous lights and powers it pushed through the dim air? Yes—even if there were no spirit of adventure among the Venuses, he would traverse and know this new world ere his friends returned. Yes; already he knew much; 'twas not a world of ocean and land, but of land and seas, or rather lakes, of high mountains and deserts. His mind reverted to their first landing, the immense waste they first rested in, and all that high barren land which lay around the northern pole of the planet, so high that it lifted itself up through the stratum of air, and to visit its wonders needed appliances as perfect as to leave the world. But it was not in these unknowable regions that J. B. Hope was interested. They had come to find a future home for the growing millions of their native earth, and here all around the tropical zone was a region fitted with everything necessary, while the dim polar regions would serve to exercise all the latent ingenuity of the coming man.

18

THE METEOR CATCHES THEM—THEY GO OUT

It was not a planet, large or small, not even a moon, but as they afterwards found of mass ably sufficient to give them a gravitation force of five ounces.

Yet it was a huge meteor coming with immense speed, large enough had it met them to crush, as [a] bullet is crushed on target, the *Star Climber*; large enough to take and carry them out on its own wild track, into the unutterable wilderness of space.

The little moon they had visited ere they had reached Venus, was a world, small perhaps; but this was but a lump, a patch, a huge curled and twisted mass of conglomerate, belched by some volcano into the outer air, a mass that would bury itself in an ocean should it ever strike a watery world, or crush a city, in a second of time, should it so happen. But, big or little, it grew out fast to their straining eyes. There was no rushing sound, not even a vibration to speak its coming, yet swiftly and inevitably it drew near.

"It will pass us," said Moxton, and then with an awful suddenness it was on them—a frightful whirl of the *Star Climber* told them they were caught and carried away captive by it, saved indeed from any sudden catastrophe, but as they again resumed their stations they saw that the *Star Climber* was dashing like a mad thing around this wandering atom. Now they saw their fierce speed, as the huge rocks sped away beneath them; and so small was the thing that held them they could feel the circular motion, the swerve, as they were swung by the invisible chain. Only Moxton's presence of mind prevented them from meeting like a comet the attracting mass, and rushing off at an elliptical orbit, every step of which would have to be, with much loss of time, retraced.

 His hand was already working the levers of their boat, the *Star Climber*'s wings were spread abroad, and those on the outside were beating the meagre air that sailed with the wandering fragment; but that alone would never have altered our headlong course—a touch of the bearer—our rocket tubes wheeled their mouths towards our huge enemy and we were conscious of the increasing distance; they burst forth—the effect was instantaneous, the head of the *Star Climber* came to, and again we were rushing around a new world. But what a world?—perhaps three miles long and one at its central diameter. But even this must have some slight atmosphere, for we were beginning to feel a great glow of heat through our vessel, and as our wings were drooped to stay our course, we could hear a roaring like a distant waterfall.

 Weir left his post of observation and stood near Moxton. The heat was growing oppressive to both.

 "We will keep as close as we can," Moxton answered to Weir. "Look!" and indeed it was needful to use all their powers to keep close to this fragment of an orb—so great their pace and so small its gravity. Round and round it they sped, and were glad to perceive their speed decreasing, and the *Star Climber* coming once more under the influence of her wings.

 There was a slight stratum of air lying in all the hollow or on the flat places, but up where its sides ran out into corners and sharp angles their course seemed as free as in space itself. They resolved to land and take a fresh departure for their home; also to survey this wandering star, and find its orbit and place, that they might not again fall into its power.

 The *Star Climber* came to rest in a long, hollow valley covered with coarse, brown sand, which seemed to have come from the corroded rocks standing up here and there amongst it, some half buried and some lying loose as if scattered there yesterday, and away on the higher ground the clear-cut, cold masses were exposed bare to the surrounding heaven.

Though they had been but ten days on their homeward journey they felt a great longing to tread on the solid ground once again, the long silent sandy slopes looked inviting, and all the higher rocks seemed to court investigation.

"Let us go out," said Weir, "if only for the fun of the thing."

Moxton agreeing, they prepared their air-pipe supplies—something like a bagpipe in appearance; they could breathe in the air through a mouthpiece and expel it through the nose. With these on they could walk in a vacuum for an hour or more.

The place where they rested was hidden from the sunbeams by a gradual rising of the ground, and Moxton suggested that Weir should step outside just to try the air and temperature.

"You can hold the door, you know, and all the thin air we get in will not hurt us."

The sliding doors were shot back and closed again behind them, then Weir opened the outer one and stepped out.

Moxton had not long to wait—the larger part of a minute, then Weir reeled in.

"What is it like?" asked his partner, as Weir panted for breath.

"What like? Well, get into an ice water bath, drink as much balloon gas as you can, and get some one to choke you, you then have an idea."

"Shall we go?"

"Oh! yes. I don't suppose it will be much worse than the shady side of the moon, and, thank heaven, it cannot blow."

"No, or it would send us into space. Don't fool about, Weir. I believe a good jump would send one clear altogether, most likely to grace this miserable fragment as a moon."

"Yes, what a fate for a bloated human, an attendant orb of the solar system, whose ambition could soar beyond. Mahomet's resting-place would be nothing to it."

"Cover up all but the eyes, Weir," said Moxton, as they were preparing.

"And those, too," answered that individual, coming out as he spoke, bound hand and foot, his glasses fastened tightly into the coverings of his face, so that the atmosphere could touch no part of his body.

Moxton followed his example; yet, ere they went, called again to Weir. "Look!" said he, putting his finger on a spring balance and lifting himself some eighteen inches from the ground.

"Yes, I see by the scale, five ounces. Well, as we have been used to weight nothing at all, we ought to get on first-rate."

So they went out together.

19

HOPE GOES WITH THE VENUSES TO FIND THEIR HOME—
SOME TIGERS FIGHT

Hyperion and Philomenia came and went freely between their own nest on the water and the dwelling place of Hope. They began to grow familiar with him and he with them. They did not show anything in their manners akin to reverence or worship; but, despite their uncouthness of aspect, they began to grow companionable. A certain individuality, probably born of long descent in a fixed type upheld and dignified them.

Unlike the enervated races of warm climes, they looked for no Avatar to pour out unthinkable blessings; no Golden Age ever shone in their distant future. They seemed to take the present time and live and think from day to day.

Hope gathered from their signs and half-comprehended words that in a far off land dwelt a nation of such as they, a Venus people, but they seemed to fear to show the way to their native country, nor could he, after once understanding them, induce them to talk on the subject. But he did not despair at the first repulse, he knew they would grow to trust him, he knew that they would soon perceive how little chance their secret had against his wondrous powers of travelling.

Never were the Venuses so content as when in their boat or on their little raft. The mainland seemed to them forbidden ground, only to be visited when necessary, and then with care and caution.

Hope began to perceive how helpless they would be against the attacks of the fiercer of the wild beasts, who probably, from finding no equal in strength, developed prodigious, if brainless, courage.

When Hope met the Venuses in the morning it was his custom to shake hands with each. This seemed entirely ludicrous to the two Venuses, and there were generally three laughter-lit faces as Hope took between his fingers the end of Hyperion's huge, muscular arm, which, from its very conformation, was incapable of any motion save a smooth, undulating one.

Then the Venuses would insist on going through their code of salutation—their long right arms would curl around Hope, then the smaller left arm would stroke in a soft, methodical manner. It usually ended by Hope's pressing his lips to Philomenia's face, which ceremony they seemed to understand, and to such an extent appreciate, that Hope had little doubt but that kissing might be easily introduced among the Venus nation.

The days, though few in number, seemed a long time to Hope, as though seasons had already passed since his comrades left him. It is ever thus. The dreary days of dull monotony appear when they are past as but an hour, while even minutes of intense feeling form often epochs in our existence. Thus it was with Hope, his long sleep was less than a dream, the hour of his awakening a whole lifetime of feeling. The many hundreds of hours passed in the *Star Climber* seemed now shorter than those fleeting seconds when he awoke and saw the Venuses.

But Hope wished to find out Venus land, and often importuned Hyperion and Philomenia to go thither, for, knowing them, he did not wish to go alone. He represented to them his power and skill, showed them the many ways in which he could aid and help, and, to accustom them to the swift motion and inure them to the new sensation, he would take them whenever they were willing short trips in his boat, the *Midge*.

One day Hope saw them conversing more earnestly together than was their practice, their faces betokening that some emotion stronger than usual was working within them. He grew anxious to know what would be the outcome. Nor had he to wait long, for they came to him and began to explain in their broken language that they wished to make some solemn covenant with him, and then show him Venus land. This was what he waited for and almost expected.

When they thought that he understood them they put each one [of] their smaller arm[s] around him and led him out of his castle till they were under the sky. Then they lifted up their right arms—huge limbs—pointing strangely to the heavens, and repeated words or made signs which, although Hope could not understand, he perceived were by them thought to be solemn and holy. At first he was quite silent, then, as they again repeated the same sounds and looked at him, and again at the sky, he perceived what they needed and tried to follow them. Perhaps he was not very successful, but his attempt pleased and tranquillized them. They loosed his arms and bowed themselves towards him, but something in their unarmed, comparatively helpless state, in their confidence and trust in him, touched Hope's heart. They would have gone at once to his aërial boat, but he stopped them. They turned and stood linked together, as was their want, before him. Then he spread out his hands and laid one lightly on each shoulder, gazing into their calm inscrutable features, his eyes going from one to the other and finding the same deep wonder in each face, the same long, patient waiting in each one's eyes.

"Listen," he said. "As long as I am with you, no harm that I can prevent shall happen to you, neither will I now or at any other time see you wronged without striving to help you, and wherever your native home may be I will always hold it a sacred thing." He ceased speaking; he took his hands from their shoulders; his eyes turned from the sky to them again. Then they all three went to the boat together.

Where would be that land, hidden from all the rude air, a valley of Avalon, shut in by mountains and deep seas, a garden of Eden, a cradle for this human-like race? They were speeding swiftly over the wood and water and the finely variegated surface of the planet, bearing a little towards the warmer regions, sometimes following long, winding, slow-paced rivers, or going above the shores of seas, flitting swiftly and silently under the directions of Hyperion and Philomenia, at a pace, indeed, vastly slower than Hope himself would travel at, for the *Midge* was built but to carry one, or at the most two, and the extra power needed to sustain the greater weight was all taken from her speed. Yet although her speed was comparatively slow, it seemed at times too great for the slow-moving brains of the two Venuses. They could only, by stopping and reconnoitring the various landmarks, proclaim the way even in an indefinite manner.

So they sped along hour after hour, Hope ever anxiously expectant to see more of these strange people, for he had gathered from Hyperion and Philomenia that they were not the only Venuses who had left their natal home, though he thought, from all that he could glean, that the number who had left were few, nor had they been happy or successful in their migrations. He looked in vain for any sign of human sense, for any raft, or hut, erected like the one he knew on the waters, for any upright form moving beneath the branching trees or on the open plain.

Troops of beasts fled away beneath him, as when, with Moxton and Weir, he had sped around the planet, and again he saw the strange sight of a huge pack of tigers spread out like a company of skirmishers, driving back a small but formidable herd of buffaloes.

Hope stopped the *Midge* and hovered over them to see the end— and that was not long in coming. The buffaloes were between the forks of a large river, and must either fight or swim. Once or twice they rushed out in a troop and seemed inclined to charge their adversaries, but were evidently afraid. Then, as they entered the broken ground, their fierce foes moved up, swiftly and silently as perfectly trained soldiers, deepening not thickening their ranks, as the ground to be guarded became less. The buffaloes gave a wild roar, half of rage and half of fear, as they saw their enemies coming nearer; then one of them leaped off into the water and swam down the stream for the other bank, all his fellows watching, even with their dull brains seeming to know his fate, for, as he neared the shore, Hope from his elevation could see three huge beasts creeping towards the spot where the buffalo would land. They allowed him to get half out of the water, then they flung themselves on him—his roar of pain being heard above the tigers' voices.

This incident was as the firing of the fuse is to the explosion; the whole of the tigers with a fearful cry rushed forward. Whether their fierce natures were roused by the cries of the strangling beast, or whether they knew that this would bring on the final rush of their victims, Hope could not tell; each and all seemed to move simultaneously. The buffaloes wheeled short round, and crushing themselves together dashed out at their foes, not singling them out individually, but evidently trying to go through them. Nor were the tigers eager to meet their direct charge, escaping often by a tremendous spring at the last moment, or, when too much before the centre of the herd to escape, bounding with a sure aim upon the back of one of the foremost. Meanwhile, like a troop of horses, from each side the tigers dashed in on the flanks at this forlorn hope. For a moment Hope thought some of the foremost would by their speed escape; but this was not to be. He already saw dashing across at a short angle about a dozen tigers which had evidently not gone far in the first rush. The three leaders, which were all that escaped the first slaughter, gave a great helpless roar as they saw their foes again upon them, then they sank to the ground beneath the teeth and claws of the victors, and as the last one fell Hope saw one of the tigers go out from the others on to a little rising ground and then give a loud, far-sounding cry—and from the side of the water and far back in the broken ground there appeared tigers answering the voice and coming to the slaughter.

EXPLORING THE WONDER

Weir and Moxton descended from the port of the *Star Climber*, and stepped out on to the surface of the meteoric mass on which their vessel now rested. It would be very safe to say that no living foot ere this had ever trodden this fragment of a world; the brown sand despite their light weight seemed like quicksilver about their feet, shifting, and seemingly flowing in an unnatural manner. Overhead stretched an inky purple sky, pierced with pale points of light, little, faint white stars. The sun was hidden from them, and the planet they had left shone like a miniature moon—a pale crescent. In the far far distance, no life or sign of life was near them. Through all their wraps they felt the penetrating cold, they realized perhaps for a second their intense isolation, their wondrous solitude, their seemingly perilous position—going away through space on a desolate frozen fragment, being carried they knew not whither, and between them and their fate stood but their aërial boat, the *Star Climber*. They were looking at her now, her blackened blistered sides, her frayed and folded pinions. Moxton drew out the point of one of them, it was the same as when they left Venus; nothing had harmed the vessel since she had passed through the Magellan cloud. They walked round her, and Moxton, going up to her prow, taking the rise of her keel in his hands, found that he could with ease lift or move her hundred tons of weight. The strangeness of all things seemed to grow on them, the thin air caused every fluid and solid in their bodies to swell and dilate, their skins grew tight, a sensation of puffiness pervaded and grew on them, their brain seemed to wander, their thoughts grew vague and uncertain, nothing seemed of the least consequence; it was as though they had drunk some ethereal champagne, and scarcely knew whether they were wandering atoms, whose home was space and whose meat and drink the thin air that stretched from star to star, or human beings who needed warmth, and food, and covering.

They knew themselves to be walking as men in a dream, beset with dangers which they could not realize. Yet in spite of all this, in spite of the uselessness of their undertaking, they both determined to persevere and fulfil the programme they had mentally sketched ere leaving the *Star Climber*.

They had intended to walk away across the sandy valley up to a ridge of rocks about half a mile distant, from which they would be able to survey at least one half of the body they were standing on.

Weir touched Moxton, who turned towards him. He took his arm and they strode away together.

As they ascended the rising ground, which had cast a shadow over them, they felt the warmth increase sensibly. The dry sand and rocks caught and retained the radiant heat, and made them well-nigh comfortable, could they have got rid of that strange, swollen, drunken-like feeling which possessed them, but this they felt to be increasing, as they hurried on to reach the rising ledge which was before them.

The soft sand yielded and flew away behind them as from the feet of an ostrich, and their stride, ostrich-like, with the least exertion carrying them many more yards than on either planet they could compass feet, brought them quickly to their destination—but not too soon. Weir was already feeling more and more uneasy; the thin air seemed mixing with their blood, and working down into the capillary tubes of their veins, though in truth it was not what they swallowed but its effects on their exterior parts which was now troubling them. Weir's fingers amid their thick wraps seemed like huge rigid bars, feeling to him more like the claws of the devil in some mediaeval painting than aught else that can be imagined. Moxton too, was suffering, but more from light-headedness. Curiosity, however, and a certain stubbornness, impelled them both to try and complete what they had mentally planned ere they left the *Star Climber*'s shelter.

But what a sight awaited them! This must surely be the very spot where Milton's devils fell—with hideous ruin and confusion—down; only the bright sun never shone there, for now beneath them was a clear precipice, not of hundreds or thousands of feet, or miles, but down, down, down beyond the lower edge of the world, and still on. The only thing that broke the dream was the vision of stars far away in the immense depth below, which the mile of barren rock seemed to emphasise—to make space gape like the mouth of hell, till to the disordered imagination those pale points of light might seem starry gleams from the great charnel house which old-world fables have built below.

The thin air seemed to have lifted from the brain of Weir and Moxton that rich harvest which the past centuries had so abundantly borne. The solid truths and fruitful facts which have so cheered ripening manhood on its way, seemed to have ascended from their brain, and from its deeper recesses arose unbidden a host of those wild thoughts which made men or women angels or devils, and drove humanity mad; their imaginations raced away and their fancies ran riot amid monstrosities as strange as any mediaeval legend. Had some fiend descended before them, they would scarce have wondered; had some aged Satyr or unlovely Faun accosted them they would not have been surprised; and then, they felt themselves to be so light, so pitiably unstable, ah! far lighter than those poor ghosts whom Dante saw driven before the more than pitiless blast!

It may be that gazing down into that immense depth affected their already benumbed brain, as a nightmare does, or as rushing water or a steep place affects the would-be suicide. They sat down on the gray rocks that were scattered around, and tried to collect their thoughts, their eyes wandering once more over the weird landscape. Away in the valley lay the *Star Climber*, black and sere, a ghostly-looking craft, the wan sun, the faint stars, the dark sky, the crumbling rocks, the loose sand—all melancholy and unnatural, as of a world in its dissolution. Yet, as they rested, their senses returned to them somewhat, and they determined to take one more look over the precipice and then return to their vessel.

They climbed on to a projecting part of the ridge, where the rocks overhung many feet, and as they gazed down the same mad thought occurred to each, namely, to cast down the cliff one of the loose rocks. 'Twas little more than the gratification of a childish whim, and Weir was naturally the more eager to fulfil it. 'Tis probable some secondary thoughts occurred to both as to how the powers of gravity would deal with the falling mass, yet their main idea was but to see a mass of rock fall clattering into the void of space. Weir was searching along the cliff trying each rock till he came to a loose one, then he nodded to Moxton to watch the effect, and with both his hands gave it a heavy push. With a dull rumble it gave way and launched itself into space—but not alone; rooted like a giant tooth along the ridge of the precipice, the huge fang had risen beneath Weir and tossed him far into space.

Moxton was transfixed that instant. Weir's fall renewed all the horrors of imagination, and paralysed his friend's mind.

Weir weighed five ounces, and the rock perhaps a thousand times as much. The impetus he gave it, unchecked by any appreciable gravity, had tossed him far into space. Moxton saw him with arms wide-spread falling, falling and turning—good God! Would he never cease to fall? The huge rock fell and struck, and fell again—but Weir out in space. Moxton thought his brain would burst. Would Weir never cease to fall?

SWIFT FALLS THE CLOUDY CURTAIN

Swift falls the cloudy curtain,
The rain comes down again,
The wild wind echoes deathfully
Across the midnight plain.

Darkness and dreary tempest
Blot out all hope of light.
No dream of joy or gladness
Breaks through the dull hours' flight.

High in a dim room lying,
Is a maid sick unto death;
She hears the wind's voice crying
With hopeless, helpless breath.

Pale—pale and sick all nature;
Weary both walls and blinds;
Helpless the eye that looks adown,
And the face she never finds.

Pale—pale and sick all nature—
All things that round her lie;
And no hope in her anguish,
For to-morrow she will die.

LOVE SONG

Daintily, O! daintily,
So daintily she goes;
Day's uncertain, night is nothing;
Time, a very wind that blows.

Wishful Eden, bless'd minute,
Can I ever linger near?
Dies the crowd's uncertain murmur
In my heedless, drunken ear.

Tell of voices, tell of breezes,
Noise of brooks in desert lands;
Dream, that thirsty wanderer pleases,
Stretched upon the shadeless sands.

But that voice by love enchanted,
Steals, ah! floats into my soul,
Wordless rapture, speechless feeling,
O'er my heart from pole to pole.

IN THE BISON FRONTIERS OF IMAGINATION SERIES

Gullivar of Mars
By Edwin L. Arnold
Introduced by
Richard A. Lupoff
Afterword by
Gary Hoppenstand

A Journey in Other Worlds:
A Romance of the Future
By John Jacob Astor
Introduced by S. M. Stirling

Queen of Atlantis
By Pierre Benoit
Afterword by Hugo Frey

The Wonder
By J. D. Beresford
Introduced by Jack L. Chalker

Voices of Vision:
Creators of Science Fiction
and Fantasy Speak
By Jayme Lynn Blaschke

At the Earth's Core
By Edgar Rice Burroughs
Introduced by
Gregory A. Benford
Afterword by Phillip R. Burger

Back to the Stone Age
By Edgar Rice Burroughs
Introduced by Gary Dunham

Beyond Thirty
By Edgar Rice Burroughs
Introduced by David Brin
Essays by Phillip R. Burger
and Richard A. Lupoff

The Eternal Savage:
Nu of the Niocene
By Edgar Rice Burroughs
Introduced by Tom Deitz

Land of Terror
By Edgar Rice Burroughs
Introduced by Anne Harris

The Land That Time Forgot
By Edgar Rice Burroughs
Introduced by Mike Resnick

Lost on Venus
By Edgar Rice Burroughs
Introduced by
Kevin J. Anderson

The Moon Maid:
Complete and Restored
By Edgar Rice Burroughs
Introduced by Terry Bisson

Pellucidar
By Edgar Rice Burroughs
Introduced by Jack McDevitt
Afterword by Phillip R. Burger

Pirates of Venus
By Edgar Rice Burroughs
Introduced by F. Paul Wilson
Afterword by Phillip R. Burger

Savage Pellucidar
By Edgar Rice Burroughs
Introduced by
Harry Turtledove

Tanar of Pellucidar
By Edgar Rice Burroughs
Introduced by Paul Cook

Tarzan at the Earth's Core
By Edgar Rice Burroughs
Introduced by Sean McMullen

Under the Moons of Mars
By Edgar Rice Burroughs
Introduced by James P. Hogan

The Absolute at Large
By Karel Čapek
Introduced by Stephen Baxter

The Girl in the Golden Atom
By Ray Cummings
Introduced by Jack Williamson

The Poison Belt:
Being an Account of
Another Amazing Adventure
of Professor Challenger
By Sir Arthur Conan Doyle
Introduced by Katya Reimann

Tarzan Alive
By Philip José Farmer
New Foreword by
Win Scott Eckert
Introduced by Mike Resnick

The Circus of Dr. Lao
By Charles G. Finney
Introduced by John Marco

*Omega: The Last Days
of the World*
By Camille Flammarion
Introduced by
Robert Silverberg

Ralph 124C 41+
By Hugo Gernsback
Introduced by Jack Williamson

*The Journey of Niels Klim
to the World Underground*
By Ludvig Holberg
Introduced and edited by
James I. McNelis Jr.
Preface by Peter Fitting

*The Lost Continent:
The Story of Atlantis*
By C. J. Cutcliffe Hyne
Introduced by
Harry Turtledove
Afterword by
Gary Hoppenstand

*The Great Romance:
A Rediscovered
Utopian Adventure*
By The Inhabitant
Edited by Dominic Alessio

Mizora: A World of Women
By Mary E. Bradley Lane
Introduced by
Joan Saberhagen

A Voyage to Arcturus
By David Lindsay
Introduced by John Clute

Before Adam
By Jack London
Introduced by
Dennis L. McKiernan

Fantastic Tales
By Jack London
Edited by Dale L. Walker

Master of Adventure:
The Worlds of
Edgar Rice Burroughs
By Richard A. Lupoff
With an introduction to
the Bison Books Edition
by the author
Foreword by
Michael Moorcock
Preface by Henry Hardy Heins
With an essay by
Phillip R. Burger

The Moon Pool
By A. Merritt
Introduced by
Robert Silverberg

The Purple Cloud
By M. P. Shiel
Introduced by John Clute

Lost Worlds
By Clark Ashton Smith
Introduced by Jeff VanderMeer

Out of Space and Time
By Clark Ashton Smith
Introduced by Jeff VanderMeer

The Skylark of Space
By E. E. "Doc" Smith
Introduced by Vernor Vinge

Skylark Three
By E. E. "Doc" Smith
Introduced by Jack Williamson

The Nightmare and Other
Tales of Dark Fantasy
By Francis Stevens
Edited and introduced by
Gary Hoppenstand

Tales of Wonder
By Mark Twain
Edited, introduced, and with
notes by David Ketterer

The Chase of the Golden Meteor
By Jules Verne
Introduced by
Gregory A. Benford

The Golden Volcano:
The First English Translation
of Verne's Original Manuscript
By Jules Verne
Translated and edited by
Edward Baxter

Lighthouse at the End
of the World:
The First English Translation
of Verne's Original Manuscript
By Jules Verne
Translated and edited by
William Butcher

The Meteor Hunt: The
First English Translation of
Verne's Original Manuscript
By Jules Verne
Translated and edited by
Frederick Paul Walter and
Walter James Miller

The Croquet Player
By H. G. Wells
Afterword by John Huntington

In the Days of the Comet
By H. G. Wells
Introduced by Ben Bova

The Last War:
A World Set Free
By H. G. Wells
Introduced by Greg Bear

The Sleeper Awakes
By H. G. Wells
Introduced by
J. Gregory Keyes
Afterword by
Gareth Davies-Morris

The War in the Air
By H. G. Wells
Introduced by Dave Duncan

The Disappearance
By Philip Wylie
Introduced by
Robert Silverberg

Gladiator
By Philip Wylie
Introduced by Janny Wurts

When Worlds Collide
By Philip Wylie and
Edwin Balmer
Introduced by John Varley